Some people are just born

UNSETTLED

HALLE

Cover Design: Vicious Desires Design
Editing: Ms. K Edits
Proofreading: Nice Girl Naughty Edits
Formatting: AJ Wolf Graphics

I live each moment as if it's your last

- creepy romance

The first murder sent shock waves through the city.

The second one had everyone scared to leave their homes.

The third caught the attention of the nation, the whisper of butterfly kisses flying across the headlines of every major newspaper.

The small town of Rivercrest Landing had a serial killer.

And in the midst of all of it, I've gotten myself tangled with a cruel boy whose cornflower eyes taunt my inner demons with the taste of his.

A boy who makes me question everything.

If I'm not careful, I might just get a butterfly kiss of my own.

Papilio machaon
Swallowtail

Callophrys rubi
White Admiral

Callophrys rub
Green Hairstreak

Celastrina argiolus
Holly Blue

Thecla betulae
Brown Hairstreak

Pyronia tithonus
Gatekeeper

Aglais io
Peacock Butterfly

Vanessa carduii
Painted Lady

ONE

butterfly kisses

MY fingertips brush along my little butterfly's jaw, moving across her cheekbone to tuck a stray piece of hair behind her ear. Pink flushes her cheeks as she lowers her emerald gaze to the red Solo cup clutched in her hand, her fingers crinkling the middle with little divots. It's obvious she doesn't get this kind of attention often.

That works in my favor.

She told me her name hours ago, but I didn't care enough to listen. I came to this party with only one purpose, and making friends was not it.

My hand leaves her hair to skim along the soft

skin of her thigh, my lips twisting into a small smirk at the little jump she does at the unexpected touch. She's a shy little thing, more of a wallflower than the other girls I've noticed.

I knew she was my *Papilio machaon*, the moment I laid eyes on her. Her golden hair matched the beautiful hue of a swallowtail's wings, the buttery strands blowing in the breeze, begging me to reach out and grab them. I had resisted, of course, but I knew at that moment that she was meant for me. She was mine to keep and to love, to adore inside of my collection.

Giving her leg a light squeeze, I bend slightly to look into her face; the movement drawing her eyes back to me. "Dance with me?" Biting her bottom lip, she gives a slight nod at my question, pink blooming across her cheeks again. My heart thumps at her response, blood pumping below my skin as I verify her answer. "Yea?"

She nods again, more exaggerated this time. "Yes." It's breathy and unsure, a sweet little whisper that makes my pulse pick up another notch with anticipation.

I carefully peel her fingers from her cup and set it aside, keeping my smile in place to prevent her from vanishing. My fingertips lightly graze her palm to link our fingers, urging her from her seat and tugging her behind me toward the middle of the room before she can change her mind. The music is some mainstream pop hit with a loud beat, something I've never heard, nor care to remember. The surrounding bodies are all swaying and grinding in the dark room, other drunken students laughing and whispering among us. The lights are low enough to give an illusion of privacy as I tug her body close, fitting her back to my front as I move my hips in time with hers.

Her skin is buzzing with nervous energy, her shoulders stiff as my trembling fingers move in to palm her waist—her innocence is intoxicating.

Bring her upstairs.

3

Take her outside.

Get her alone.

The thoughts nag at the back of my skull, pushing me to hurry things along, but I shake my head, forcing myself to concentrate.

She's the high I want to bottle up, to store her memory like a keepsake to look back on. My chin tickles as she moves, the flowery smell of her hair teasing my nostrils as it brushes against me. Creeping my hands along her sides as she dances, I smile against her skin at the shiver that shakes up her spine. Dropping my face to skim my lips over her exposed shoulders, I trail them on her skin to speak into her ear. "Relax. We're just dancing."

Resting a palm on her bare midriff, I let the edge of my fingers brush the top of her waistband as she settles back into me again, a shy little look cast over her shoulder. "We don't have to just dance." It's so low I almost don't hear it over the music, almost like she's embarrassed the words ever left her pretty little red mouth.

I don't have to be in the light to know she's blushing again, my eager little butterfly. Looks like I'm not the only one wanting to get things rolling. I won't let her brave little words go to waste. "You have a room here?"

Her smile widening, she gives me another small nod and I beam at her.

Thump thump.

Thump thump.

Thump thump.

I almost can't focus over the whooshing of my pulse in my ears.

She takes my hand, her fingers softly grasping mine, and our eye contact breaks as she glances around the room. Moving through the crowd and up the stairs, I watch her back, eyes catching on the slight sway of her golden hair as she moves. Each step takes us further from the party below, my breaths increasing in their intensity with each place of my foot. Closing my eyes for a brief moment, I squeeze my vacant hand in a fist, focusing on the pinch in my knuckles to gain control.

Chewing her lip, she opens a door at the end of the hall, watching me through her lashes. I pull my fingers from hers and walk into the room. "Sorry it's a little messy, I wa—"

I spin and cut her off mid-sentence, yanking her mouth to mine in an aggressive smack of lips. Mentally calming myself, I soften the kiss while using my body to guide her backward, pressing her back against the door to shut it. Palming her face, I suck her bottom lip into my mouth, letting it slip through my teeth with a gentle, wet pop. "I don't care about the mess."

Her breath fans over my damp lips, quick little puffs that have my hands trembling again. Pulling her mouth back to mine, I pick up where I left off, my tongue running over hers to hide the impatient shake of my fingers. She tastes sweet like honey, a hint of Jack Daniels burning across my tongue with each swipe that passes through her teeth.

I want to suck the taste from her mouth until there's nothing left to taste and run my fingers through the yellow of her hair until I can't feel my fingertips and the color bleeds from the strands. I want to burn her touch into my skin, take everything from her and make it mine. She will be only mine to remember. My little *Papilio machaon* pinned to my wall by the torn edges of her golden wings. Tattered and defeated, but so fucking beautiful in all her disheveled glory.

My fingers trail along her skin, catching onto the fabric of her shirt as I move down her body, brushing along the brass of the denim buttons on her jeans as they move to press along the seam of her pussy. My lips part against her mouth in a pleased smile as I press into the heat between her legs. My little butterfly is more than ready for me, so hot I can practically feel the damp pool gathering in her panties through the thick denim.

I tighten my grip in her hair with my free hand, her little gasp of surprised pleasure wrapping around my heart beneath my ribs.

I want more.

I need more.

Turning us, I move her toward her bed, my lips twisting into a smirk at another gasp that slips from her chest when I push her back onto the pillows and climb up and over her body. My eyes burn over her as I watch her watch me, my tongue reaching out to run a wet path along her exposed belly. Her eyes close when my tongue dips to taste the flesh just under her waistband, and I reach behind my back to pull out the cotton binding I stuffed into my back pocket earlier. The soft fabric teases my fingers as I grip it in my fist, my belly growing hot with my own arousal.

My lips latch onto her skin as I move up her body, nose pushing along the edge of her shirt to kiss along the valley of her breasts. The fabric rises with me, and I sit back just a bit, admiring the swell of her big, beautiful tits as they heave with her excitement, the rose pink of her nipples straining against the soft mesh of her bra.

My butterfly is so fucking beautiful.

My fingers tickling up the length of her arms, I keep the binding tucked into my palm, guiding her arms so that they're pressed to her sides. I shift forward just the slightest bit in case she tries to fight me, pinning her limbs with my knees. My head drops to suck one of her tight rosy buds into my mouth through the thin mesh of her bra, running the tip of my tongue along its stiff tip. She looks beautiful from this position, helpless, at my mercy. Coming back to her mouth, I press a slow lingering kiss to her sweet lips, fingers shaking as I wrap my bind behind her head, fingertips catching onto a few stray strands of her golden hair.

Trailing kisses from her lips to her ear, my hand returns between her legs, palm pressing roughly over the bud of her clit through the rough fabric of her denim. The brass buttons dig into my wrist as I create the friction her thrusting hips are looking for. "Keep your eyes closed."

She nods almost aimlessly, lashes fluttering against her cheeks as she chews on her bottom lip with pleasure. I pull my hand away, eyes trained on the flush of her skin, the white mark on her lip from her teeth. Grabbing the loose ends of my bind, I quickly tie off the gag over her mouth, smiling at the little frown that creases her brow. My fingers run over her lips through the bind as she mumbles out muffled words that I can't make out. Her eyes are open now, but at the slight shake of my head, she refrains from any possible fight.

Ever the trusting little butterfly.

A familiar warmth is blooming in my chest, the comforting ache wrapping around my heart as my lungs press out quickening breaths. My heart bangs in my ears as I pull out another tie, making a show of it for my butterfly. I run it through my fingers and trail the end of it along her belly, over her nipples. I smile as she arches under the whisper of a touch, her skin flushed and pebbled with arousal. This is a game to her as much as it is to me, and that sends a thrumming of annoyance through my blood. Although easier, it's so much more fun when they fight.

The cotton over her lips is damp from her breath, the red of her lipstick shining through to tease and tempt me as I bring her arms up one at a time to rest above her head. She blinks up at me as I sweetly kiss the tender flesh of her wrist, wrapping my bind around them to tie her to the metal of her bed frame. Unable to resist any longer, I dip down and kiss her through the bind, the feel of the fabric across my tongue beating a rhythm between my legs. The sweet little whimpers leaking through almost have my own hips shifting, the knowledge of what's coming burning hot in my gut.

Lips still on hers, my little butterfly doesn't notice the sharp press of my knife slicing a long line from her wrist to elbow until I pull away. Her eyes widen in confusion as she blinks at the bloody tip, the slight quizzical tremble of her chin taking all my attention as I slice another long line along her other arm. It takes a moment for her blood to well up, but when it does, the fat, dark, tear-shaped drops that slide down her arms come in thick spurts that trickle onto her shoulders, sliding over her ivory skin to stain the yellow blond of her hair the prettiest shade of red.

I get lost in the hue, the rich berry of it painting her pillow with every shake of her little head. Her golden wings are losing their dust as she thrashes below my hips, the soft, weak edges tearing as they get stained with red. She's so, so beautiful. More beautiful than I thought she could ever be. Her screams are muffled through the bind, and I almost reach forward, fingers curling into my palm above her face to stop myself. Not that anyone would hear her over the music downstairs, but that's too risky.

Crystal clear tears leak down her cheeks, deep water pools of seafoam pleading to a lost cause as she stares up at me, brows pinched to match the frown of her crying lips. Uncurling my hand, I use a single fingertip to wipe one of her tears away, the wet drop stirring a whirlwind in my gut as I bring the lone drop to my lips to lick the salt away. Only spending another moment to watch her, I reach back into my pocket and pull out a small paper butterfly.

Its yellow edges are crinkled from being stuffed away, but it's okay; it's just like my perfect little butterfly. I don't smooth out the edges. Instead, I let it stay rumpled, watching its little paper wings flap and fly along her skin with each heaving breath that leaves her chest. When my little butterfly's eyes become droopy, I move my attention to her pretty little face, swallowing as her body twitches beneath me in a last-ditch effort to save herself, paper butterfly wings flapping one last time as she takes her final shaking, shallow breath.

That's always my favorite part. Those last few moments before they die. Their body has so much to say in those last few seconds, and I savor every silent word, store every painful whisper inside my heart, and watch the light leave behind nothing but a shell to rot.

Reluctantly shifting off of her, I wipe the blood from the tip of my knife onto her stained pillowcase, carefully tucking it away as I brush off my own clothing. Triple checking for any stray droplets of blood, I take the time needed to make sure I'm clean. Satisfied, I look down at my beautiful butterfly and run my fingertips over her cheek in a whisper of a touch that burns the very tips of my fingers. Closing my eyes to stop myself from staying any longer, I burn her image into my memory, pressing all of her into that bottle of memories, then slip out of her door and into the hall, quietly clicking it shut behind me. Taking a shallow breath, I retreat down into the main house, grabbing a stray drink off of a table as I pass. Inserting myself into a near group, I fake a laugh as someone tells a joke I missed the beginning of, flawlessly immersing myself back into the fray like I had never left.

Hours tick by as I continue to mingle, the shaking of my fingers lessening as my high slips away with the hands of the clock. The fallout gets worse every time, the high never lasting quite as long as the last. A fact I'm finding both annoying and alarming. It's just after two a.m., my arm poised back as I play beer pong, when a bone-chilling shriek leaks down the stairs and into the party. I crunch the plastic beer pong ball between my fingers as confused chaos ensues, girls screaming from the stairs that my butterfly is dead. I smile into my cup, using it to hide the expression stretching across my cheeks as I revel in my secret for the briefest of moments. It bleeds over all the music, waves of panic spreading throughout everyone. The lights cut on and the music pauses, students starting to buzz as the news starts to travel.

Several of the students around me are sobbing into their phones, a pair of frat boys blocking the entrance to the stairs to prevent anyone from going up. It's only a matter of time before the authorities will show up. I let a girl next to me grab my arm, her cries burying inside of my chest as she tugs us toward the exit, her tears streaking mascara down her cheeks. Following the dispersing crowds, we stand outside of the sorority house, blue-and-red lights blinking down the street as they come speeding up toward the lawn. Using the scattering partygoers as cover, I duck off and out of sight before the police pull into the drive, sliding my hoodie up over my head as I step into the shadows.

My hands tuck into my pockets as I walk back to the car I parked down the street, the shadows of the night hiding the smile I let out now that I'm alone. My little butterfly will be all over the news in the morning, and I have my television set to record.

TWO

hadley

My body jolts forward at the sharp smack that lands on my ass, my palms digging into the bedsheets to keep myself from sliding forward. "You like that, baby?" Another smack and one of my hands moves to brace against the headboard, my lips pinching as hot breath meets my ear. "Yea, you do. You love it, don't you? You dirty little slut."

My eyes twitch as I fight from rolling them, a low breath parting my lips as I give him the answer I know he wants. "Oh yea, you're so

He's oblivious to the insincerity lacing my tone, or the bored expression that's been on my face since we started this evening's charade, as usual, my little lie spurring him into a frenzy of grunts and unrestrained thrusts that rock me further into his mattress. My gaze raises from the sheets to my hand still braced on the headboard, ears blocking out the squeaking of the springs and the soft, sweet scent of another woman's perfume wafting from the fabric beneath me. My eyes find the oval mood stone nestled between various other silver pieces of jewelry on my middle finger. The stone's smooth surface is mixed with gray and white, little swirls of hollowness reflecting my inner thoughts in the glint of the pale moonlight that shines through the crack of the curtains covering the window.

That's a feeling I don't need my ring for, though. It's as familiar as the pang of disappointment that burns along my ribs whenever I think of Nana, as constant as the sorrow that paints my heart with ugly strokes of blue-gray misery. A gift from her, the mood ring was one of her many solutions to my problems. She had a solution for everything. I never had a problem that she didn't have an answer for. Granted, her solutions rarely worked for me, but that's hardly her fault. My problems run a little deeper than most.

This particular one, though, did work. I've always been unsure of my own feelings. My ring helps me feel grounded. I don't necessarily need it now. As I got older, it wasn't as necessary as when I was a kid, but I still want it, for both sentimental reasons and as a guide.

Most days, I know I'm decidedly not okay without looking at it. Nana always said, *Hadley, the day is what you make of it, honey, and you can make it great.* She said it like it was a simple solution, to just not have a bad day, to just not be sad. And maybe it is that simple. Nana certainly was never sad.

But Nana isn't here anymore, and all I have of her is my ring and memories that make it swirl gray and yellow. I am nothing but a broken doll without her. A puppet for those around me to use as they see fit, jerk around even as my strings fray from the constant abuse and my porcelain cracks. I have no one that truly cares about me. I'm just the sad, quiet girl who relies on an old pawn shop ring to tell me how I'm feeling. The girl who lets guys fuck her to feel a semblance of intimacy inside her cold, dark world of self-doubt. Their rough hands and wet lips never quite fill that void, not completely, but for a few precious moments, I can pretend.

I can pretend I'm not the girl who fucks strangers in the dark, so they don't see my scars. That I'm not the girl who cries into her pillow over the pain in her chest she doesn't understand. That I'm not the girl who has nothing and no one. I desperately want to be wanted, not just for my body, but for me. I desperately want to be needed in a way that doesn't involve sex or a means to an end. But if my past has taught me anything, it's that that's not the life I've been given. I drew the short end of the stick, destined to be the black sheep, branded with the mark of disgrace for all to see.

At some point, I know I'll stop chasing my need to feel needed, that I'll just give up and disappear like everyone I've ever cared about. But right now, I'm still sick with lust for it. My desperate heart makes me sick even as I do what I have to, to feed that dark pit that lives just under my ribs. I hate that I allow myself to be used. I hate that I allow my strings to be stroked and plucked at the will of others. I hate that I like it. I hate that a dark, sick part of me clings to it, because it's all I can get.

Kyler's body lands atop mine as he orgasms; hot, sticky ropes of cum dripping down the inside of my thighs as he pulls out of me to spray his release across my ass cheeks. He does it for his own satisfaction, something he's never voiced, but I'm more than aware of as his fingers swipe over the warmth of it to swipe a sticky path down the crease of my ass.

I'm not worried about getting pregnant; I had an emergency hysterectomy when I was fourteen. I was too young to care at the time to know exactly what that meant, to know that I'd never be able to have my own children, but I knew it was significant based on how all the adults would get the same look on their face whenever they found out. How they all would look down on me with what I now realize was pity. A look my parents never had on theirs, I might add. As I got older, I never felt sad about it; instead, my ring only ever glows violet with happiness when I think about it. I am not fit to be a mother. That I know, without a doubt. I would never wish to bring another being into this awful world. A thought I wish my parents had before forcing me into it. Although, I often think they thought the same, but for different reasons.

I rest my cheek against Kyler's pillow as his weight presses into me, feeling so heavy it's almost difficult to breathe. I don't mind, though. If anything, I almost wish I couldn't at all. "You came, baby?" I swallow, closing my eyes with the hum that I force past my lips in answer to his question. Of course I didn't. I almost never do, but telling him that would be pointless. He kisses the side of my head and I feel my heart flutter at the contact, the need for those types of touches pulling my aching heart by its sad little strings. "Good."

He moves from me, and his warmth is immediately replaced by the cool breeze of the air conditioner sitting in the window, my skin pebbling under the direct contact. My eyes open just enough to track his dark form as he walks to the bathroom, and I stay lying on the bed until the door shuts behind him, watching the light flick on under the crack of the door. Ignoring the yellow swirling in my ring, I rise from the bed, using his own sheets to clean my legs and ass. Reaching down, I grab my underwear off the floor and tug them on, quickly covering my skin with my discarded clothing. I slip my dirty, old converse onto my feet as I build my armor back up before Kyler gets out of the bathroom.

The soft glow from the bathroom lights up his room as he comes out, now in a pair of black-fitted briefs. He frowns at me as I grab my phone from his nightstand, his warm brown orbs settling on my face, when I turn to look at him. "You know you can stay."

He steps forward, his hand reaching out to touch my cheek, but I step to the side and watch his arm fall. I know I can stay. The needy, desperate part of me wants that; wants to let him hold me all night, but the logical, sane part of me doesn't. I don't want that. I don't want to need that. Kyler doesn't love me. He doesn't actually have any genuine feelings for me. He only calls me when his girlfriend is out of town, only acknowledges me when it's convenient for him. I allow myself to come here to fill that void, but I won't allow that weakness to take over. I already hate that I'm here, hate that I let him use me.

I step around him, my fingertips trailing along the wall as I put space between us. I can feel his gaze follow me in the dark as I walk across his small studio apartment, the soft sound of my feet sinking into his carpet the only noise. I look over my shoulder as I open the door, the security light from the complex hallway flooding into the space. "Tell Vickie hi for me."

He snorts at the mention of his girlfriend, shaking his head with an unamused smirk. He starts to speak but I don't listen, shutting the door before he's finished. It's late, maybe close to three a.m., so I'm the only one on the street when I leave his complex. Tucking my hands into the pockets of my hoodie, I step off the sidewalk, choosing to walk through the dark park. I should stay on the lighted walkway, but I don't, stepping off into the grass instead, licking my lips as the warm summer night breeze blows my hood off of my head.

My feet pause in the grass momentarily, eyes falling on to the sleeping bag nestled against some outstretched branches of an overgrown bush. Not wanting to bother the poor man's sleep, I head in the other direction. Seeing another person reminds me that I'm not alone, despite the stillness that fills the park at this hour. My thoughts wander to the recent news headline that I'd read just the other morning, the title inky and dark next to the blurry photo of a pretty blonde woman. Ella Rosenberg, the article had said, was a junior at Lancaster University, majoring in economics and was a part-time ballet instructor at the local dance school. Her light was snubbed out at a university party where she was murdered in her sorority bedroom, left with nothing but bloody sheets and a butterfly kiss. That's what the locals are calling the little paper butterflies that are left behind with every slayed soul, anyway.

What a pretty name they've given something so ugly.

An arm wraps around my head, a hand slapping over my mouth and stopping my forward progression as I suck in a surprised gasp. My heart pumps in my ears as lips brush along my cheek in a familiar touch that does nothing but spur it to beat even harder against my ribs. "Got you."

Rhys's fingers dip between my lips as he pulls his hand away, pressing the tips into my teeth as they push into the soft flesh. I fight the urge to slip my tongue between my teeth and taste his fingertips, letting their rough pads brush more than the inside of my lips. I may have left Kyler's house less than twenty minutes ago, but unlike him, Rhys is the forbidden fruit I crave. He terrifies me in a way I don't understand and makes me feel things that my mood ring doesn't show me. Around him, I forget everything I've grown to understand about myself, constantly eyeing my ring to tell me how I feel.

Right now, the dark pink and purple swirls glinting in the low lights tell me I'm more than just happy to see him. He excites me. Makes me drunk with lust.

Rhys Elliot is everything that I'm not, everything I wish I was and also not. He's an enigma to me in the same aspect that I understand him completely. He has friends, real ones, who actually want him around. He's not afraid to say what's on his mind or stand up for himself. He radiates an energy that everyone is drawn to, like moths to the soft blue haze of a bug zapper. But unlike the others, that's not what draws me. No, I crave to see the way his cornflower eyes burn when he gets angry. To see the shadow of his face when he lets his demons take the forefront. He holds his shadows close in his chest, just like I do, fighting the urge to let them loose. His ugly reminds me that I'm not the only one.

Yet despite the inky fingers of his darkness gripping his ankles, he can still radiate the light needed to illuminate the room. He can still smile so wide that all you see is nothing but perfectly straight teeth. Rhys has found a way to still be happy, and I find myself eyeing the green of my mood ring whenever his smile isn't directed my way. Much to the ache of my heart, it usually isn't.

Fingers falling from my face, he moves to stand in front of me, eyes so brilliantly blue they almost shine in the dark. He's not smiling as he crowds me, fingers reaching out to grip the collar of my hoodie and tug me close. His knuckles dig into the soft skin under my chin as I look up at him, eyes blinking as his breath blows over my face. "What did I tell you about walking alone at night, Hadley?"

I swallow and his knuckles press even deeper into my throat. While everyone else gets the kind boy with an apparent hard edge, I get nothing but stone. But I wouldn't want anything else. "Not to."

My simple answer tugs a smile onto the corner of his lips, tilting them toward the pale glow of the moon as he looks down at me. It disappears almost as quickly as it came, his hand twisting the fabric at my neck to tighten it in his fist. "You were with him again, weren't you?"

Although I couldn't be sure, I almost think it makes Rhys angry that I search out comfort from others and not him. We don't have that sort of relationship, he and I, but we could. We dance along a thin line between being friends and almost lovers. Neither one of us is willing to admit we have more similarities than differences. I'd like to think he's drawn to my dark in the same way that I'm drawn to his, that the strange bond we share is because of our demons, but I don't actually know. I know that he doesn't hang out with me if he has other options, yet he seeks me out every chance he gets. I imagine he's just as confused by us as I am, and I find that thought comforting in a weird way.

I don't know how long we stand there, staring at each other, but he doesn't seem bothered by the delay in my response. "Why ask when you already know the answer?" I tilt my face the slightest bit, eyes narrowing on him. "When are you going to admit you wait out here for me? That you're hoping to get his sloppy seconds." I'm only ever brave enough to speak so boldly around Rhys, never able to find the courage in situations I actually need it.

His eyes flit across my face instead of answering, that dark of his hiding behind the blue, teasing me with just a small glimpse. I wish he didn't keep it bottled up like that. I want him to let it loose. I hate to admit that I try to get it out whenever I can, try to coax it out with my snotty quips and false anger.

I hiss as he jerks me up onto the tips of my sneakers, his teeth biting into my cheek, my toes scrunching as he scrapes across my skin to tear into my bottom lip. It's hardly a kiss, the soft flesh of my lip bleeding and my face stinging as he shoves me backward, his fingers slipping from the fabric of my hoodie as I'm pushed away from him. The heel of my sneaker catches on the grass, and I almost fall, but he grabs my arm, fingers bruising through the sleeve of my hoodie. "You're so fucking clumsy, Hadley."

I jerk my arm from his grip, my tongue swiping over my lip to wipe away the metallic sting. Rhys is cruel and rude, all wrapped up in a package so pretty that even angels would cry with jealousy at just one look at him. His back is to the glow of the moon, but I wouldn't need the small bit of light to know what the cut of his jaw looks like, how his hair is a bright peroxide blond that flops over his brow when he looks down at me. I'm fairly tall for a woman, but he's even taller, with shoulders wide enough to fill doorways. He's a beast trapped in a man's body; a horned devil stuck in the confines of a beautiful shell walking among humans.

"Are you walking me home or not?" My voice is loud in the dark, and my eyes flick to the sleeping man under the brush not far from us. I forgot he was even there. I hadn't made it very far from him when Rhys snuck up on me.

He shakes his head, strands of white-blond hair hiding his eyes from me as he starts to step backward. "Not." He spins away and I don't need my ring to know the smoke billowing around my lungs reeks of disappointment. "Oh, and Hadley?" He doesn't look back, his voice drifting over his shoulder as he keeps moving farther away from me. "Try not to get a butterfly kiss."

THREE

butterfly kisses

B reathe in.

Breathe out.

My feet lightly slap along the concrete in tune with my lungs, nostrils flaring when I push myself a fraction faster to keep pace with the ebony ponytail swinging ahead of me. Her dark head disappears beyond the bend in the path despite my quickening pace, and I bite my cheek, pushing myself to keep her in my sight.

I've been thinking about this for days. I'm not about to let her fly away now.

"Do you run here often?" Earbuds are pulled from her left ear as she tilts her face my way, eyes widening

ever so slightly at my nearness. I lift my leg up onto the park bench and tighten my shoelaces as her perfectly whitened teeth flash.

"Did you say something? Sorry, I didn't hear you." Her tongue darts out to wet her parted lips, eyes following my face as I stand and lower my foot from the bench. I don't miss the way she takes a slight step away from me.

"I just asked if you run here often. I'm new to the area and I haven't had great success finding a new running spot."

I see the moment she relaxes, fingers unflexing from the scrunched fabric of her athletic top. "Oh yea, I run almost every morning. It's great here." She gestures to her left with her thumb, her long black ponytail swinging over her shoulder with the movement. My eyes are drawn to the shiny strands, the inky black reminding me of the soft flap of a White Admiral's wings as they blow in the soft breeze. "This way ends on the east side of the park. It's my favorite because of the trees."

I stretch my arm over my chest, raising a brow at her. "The trees?"

She smiles, a small laugh scrunching up her nose in a way that makes my gut flutter. "Yea, the trees." Her lips pinch in another smile, a flirty flush marking her cheeks before she continues. "It's more secluded than the other side of the park. I don't feel like everyone is watching me there."

I nod at her, giving her a smile of my own as I look past her and down the path. "I might have to get a look at these trees of yours." Pulling the earbuds from my pockets, I put one in my ear, winking at her as I step around her. "Maybe I'll see you tomorrow?"

I had seen her the next day. And the day after. And often enough to know that she runs four days a week, although the days vary. I've been running for weeks, something I thought I'd never do, just to see her dark ponytail sway on the path ahead of me every morning. No matter what though, she *always* runs on Thursday, and just like she said the first time we met, the east path is her favorite. She never runs any other way; always shows up fifteen minutes before dawn, always takes five to eight minutes to stretch before she runs, Shakira blasting from her earbuds.

Thanks to her, I've had "Hips Don't Lie" on a loop in my head every fucking day.

We don't talk much; a few sentences at most before we separately start our exercise. We haven't even exchanged names, but it's unnecessary. I've learned everything I needed in the time we didn't talk. It takes my *Limenitis camilla*, my little black-and-white butterfly, just over forty minutes to finish her run. The last ten minutes are always spent at a more leisurely pace than the rest. She takes her time winding through the heaviest growth of trees and bushes, watching the sun finish rising through the branches.

I'll admit it took me a few days to be able to look past the decorative slits in the leggings that fit like a glove over her long legs, or the smooth curve of her slim waist. Even longer to keep my gaze off of the long, overgrown length of her ebony hair. It shines and snaps when she runs, smells sweet and floral when it catches on the breeze. I know it'd look even more beautiful wrapped around my fist. It's my favorite part of my *Limenitis camilla.*

Although everything about her is almost perfection, I can't help but feel like she's missing something. She's beautiful, but not flawless, and I know *exactly* what she needs.

The thought has me picking up my pace again, eyes lasering in on that glorious swaying hair when it comes back into view. She knows I'm here. I often run behind her, so my increased speed won't be alarming to her. The smack of my shoes on the path fills my ears as I press closer, the earbuds in my ears silent as always. I've never used them to listen to music. They're only there to give the illusion, so my little butterfly feels comfortable enough to take her personal phone calls when I'm near or mumble her favorite song

41

lyrics. She has no idea I'm privy to every conversation she's had during these last few weeks on her run and heard every off-key song.

I'm close enough now that I can hear the faint thumping of her music through her earbuds, and if I strain enough to listen, every loud inhale and exhale that leaves her chest. Every step closer has my heart thumping more roughly against my ribs, has my lungs sucking in almost too much air. My fingers bite into my palms as I pump my arms, keeping them confined within my own clutch instead of straining to touch the silk of her hair. Being this close to her always makes me shake, makes my mouth water in anticipation.

Ripping my eyes off her back, I scan the path, my feet almost losing grip with the jolt that races along my spine. We're almost to the final stretch, my little butterfly's pace starting to slow as she relaxes a bit. I choke down the knot in my tightening throat, taking a quick look behind my back as we get swallowed up by more trees, the path becoming more and more secluded with every step that's slapped onto the pavement.

I've thought about this so many times that it almost feels surreal to finally be here, in this moment. The anticipation has been gnawing at my neck like a rabid dog, ripping and tearing into my will to be patient from the second my eyes landed on my butterfly's ebony wings. The sweat slicking down my nape, dripping between my shoulder blades, scrapes along the goosebumps lining my skin. If I wanted, I could reach out and run my fingertips along the soft fabric of my *Limenitis camilla*'s shirt. I'm that close. My lips part as I mentally count down the seconds, knowing exactly how many steps it'll take us to get to a very specific curve in the path.

Four Mississippi.

The pounding in my chest is almost painful, my feet shadowing my butterfly perfectly.

Three Mississippi.

I can smell that intoxicating sweet scent of her hair, almost feel the dark strands as they wave back toward my face.

Two Mississippi.

My gaze leaves her for just a fraction of a moment, flickering between her ebony wings and the weeping willow we're coming up to.

One Mississippi.

My fingers grace along the back of her head, whispering through the strands of her hair, my fingertips burning against the soft silk before sinking into her scalp. My leg comes forward with hers, looping around the front of her shin while my elbow and hand shove her head forward. Her hair turns violent, almost slicing my fingers as she catapults toward the pavement, ebony strands burning from my palm as her face meets the ground with a wet slap and crunch that mutes the startled yelp that leaves her lips.

She slides forward on the pavement, her body momentarily scrunching like an accordion, arms, hands and face scratching along the coarse ground as an earbud flies from her ear to skip and roll off of the path. Almost heaving, I step over her moaning, writhing form, purposefully stepping onto a hand that's blindly searching the ground by her head. There's already a small splattering of blood painted across the pavement from her initial hit, abstract art spreading around to accentuate the soft fluttering of her dark wings. It's so beautiful I almost get lost in it, but her low groan draws my attention back to the task at hand, and I tug my fingerless gloves from my pocket, slipping them on as I watch her slowly wiggle under me.

I bend over to bring the end of her long, tangled ponytail to my face and take a deep breath, savoring that floral beauty until my lungs burn and I'm forced to exhale. My tongue comes out to wet my lips as I wind it around my fist, slowly wrapping it around and around and around, until it's so tight I almost can't feel my fingers. Digging into the hair at the base of the elastic, I tilt my butterfly's face up off the pavement, admiring the red and brown mixed over her beautiful features. She's making small little noises, eyes trying to fight their way open.

Fuck, I want to kiss her, taste the dirt clinging to her cheeks, lick the blood from her teeth. But this isn't about my selfish wants this time, this is all about my butterfly. I've thought long and hard about this, spent nights sweating in my sheets over the images. Today, my butterfly will finally be flawless.

She will *finally* be perfect.

Just as her eyes flutter open under my gaze, I slam her face back into the ground and watch her nose crunch and lips split even more. More blood sprays along the ground and I force myself to move my face from the prime-viewing position to hover over her back. I want to see everything, but I can't risk getting overly dirty. Lifting her face, I slam it back down again, eyes fixed on the ground, frantically shifting over the pavement to watch every spray and drop turn black where it lands.

Over and over and over, I slam her head down, blood starting to pool around her, threatening to stain the tips of my sneakers as it creeps close. Her chest stopped moving long ago, her fingers no longer scratching at the ground, legs no longer quivering between mine. She hasn't made any sounds in a long while, however I couldn't help but to keep using her as my paintbrush; stamp her into the pavement with pretty shades of red.

My hands are shaking, arms tired when I finally stop. I take my time unwrapping her ebony locks, my fingers tinted a light purple, the edges of my knuckles etched with red lines from being pinched for so long. I step back toward her legs before the red ripples surrounding her can reach me, my lips parting as I stare down at what can only be described as absolute perfection.

My butterfly's arms are fanned out from her body, one bent oddly toward herself while the other reaches past her head, palm up. Her face is flat against the pavement, perfectly fitted to every bump and ripple in the coarse ground, the blood sprayed around her almost reminiscent of a pair of torn and mangled wings. I can't help the laugh that bubbles from me, my hand coming up to cover my mouth as I smile down at her.

I knew she'd be nothing short of stunning.

I just *knew* it.

It takes me a few tries to unzip the pocket on my joggers, my hands trembling as I pull out the black-and-white origami butterfly I'd made just for her last night. I was careful when tucking it into my pocket this time. I wanted its wings to be as perfect as my butterfly. Holding it up, I cover her head from my view, the red wings stroking lovingly along the pavement wrapped around the small piece of paper. *Stunning.* Lifting my foot over her, I step off to the side, careful not to step into the growing, murky puddle that's seeping into her clothes. I bend and carefully place the butterfly in her palm, skimming my fingertips along her skin as I stand.

Pulling my eyes from her, I look down at my clothes, my hands brushing over my shirt as I feel for wetness. A small amount of red stains my fingertips when I lift them for inspection, but I shrug it off. My clothes and shoes are all black, so it's virtually impossible to see it. As long as I don't touch anything, people will just assume I'm sweaty from my run. Slowly backing away, I admire the way the early sunrays glimmer through the weeping willow's branches, how the shadows twist over my butterfly's still form.

I know I need to get back to my run, that I have maybe twenty minutes before the other routine runners come this way, but I wish I could stay all day. I wish I could sit and listen to Shakira playing from her earbud that's hidden in the grass and watch the blood dry and crust along the edges of her smooth skin. It's truly unfair how little time I get with my butterflies. Turning away, I start to run once more, my eyes fixed on the path, forcing my body to move and not turn back.

Picking up my pace, my knees almost knock together with every step that brings me closer to the end of the path. I can already feel the heat of my skin turning cold now that my butterfly is left behind. I have to remind myself that they may only be mine for a small time, face-to-face, but they live forever in my collection. And my *Limenitis camilla* will look immaculate hanging next to all the others, her dusty wings frayed along the edges and cracked down the middle.

Like anyone who collects things though, I'm never quite satisfied with what I have. I can already feel the need to start searching for my newest find, feel the tug in my chest urging me for more. But I know that can wait. I need to let my butterfly rest in her box for a bit before I move on to my next pretty. She deserves the attention after such a beautiful performance.

I break from the tree line, curving toward the east park gate. Out of breath, I lean over and palm my knees once I get to the sidewalk, my eyes briefly flicking to the side as a man comes to stand near the bus stop with me.

"Must have been a good run."

I huff at his remark, a smirk twisting my lips as I straighten, watching the bus pull in front of us. "It was perfect."

FOUR

hadley

Leaning my head back, I close my eyes as I listen to the priest across the grass. I can't actually hear exactly what he's saying, but I can hear the faint mumblings of words that drift through the space between us. Thankfully, they're behind me so I can sit here unseen, hidden with my back resting against Nana's tombstone. No one would care if they did see me here. People often visit the dead, but I'd prefer to just not be seen. I don't know exactly why I even come here. I personally don't even believe Nana is still here, floating around in this lonely graveyard, waiting for me to prattle on about my boring days. I don't know where she is, if she even is anywhere, but it's not here. Still, being close to something that belongs to her, where I'd last seen her, is comforting to me, I guess.

Opening my eyes, I stare out at the orange and purple billowing in the sky, pink clouds floating along the horizon as the sun sets. The day might be ending for most, but it's just beginning for me. I've always been a night owl, always preferred the chaotic bustle that comes after dark over the daylight traffic. There's something peaceful about being busy while others sleep.

Sneakers squish into the grass and I turn my face in the direction of the sound. Only a moment later, Rhys's scowl comes into view, his hand pulling from his jean pocket to wave for me to shift over. I oblige his silent request, scooting over to make room for him. I'm here so often that the grass has died where I sit, rubbed away so there's nothing but dirt that stains the butt of my pants.

Rhys drops down, long legs stretching in front of him as he presses into me. I turn my face away without comment, my eyes falling to the rips in his denim. Unlike the jeans you can buy, I know his were made from actual wear and tear. They're also his favorite pair, if the amount of times I've seen him in them says anything.

Reaching to my side, I grab the pair of coffee cups I'd brought with me, passing off one to Rhys while resting my own between my drawn-up knees. Finding the thermos that was sitting in the grass beside them, I unscrew the top and fill my cup to the brim before handing that over as well. I don't watch as he fills his cup, but my lips do pinch together in quiet laughter when I hear his disgusted scoff.

"Seriously, Hadley? You're so fucking weird." I look over at him in time to see his grimace as he gulps down half of his cup, his eyes narrowing on my face as I take a long, slow drink out of my own mug. The gin burns down my throat, bitter and earthy like pine needles. I think I like it because I can associate it with something I know, unlike other kinds of alcohol.

"Am I though? I'm visiting Nana and I like gin." I take another drink, smiling around the edge of my cup as he throws the rest of his back with a scrunched nose. "You're the one sitting in a graveyard without reason, chugging alcohol you don't even like. That seems weird to me."

He sets his empty cup down, his lips smacking as he leans back into the tombstone. His head tilts my way as I follow his example, gulping back the rest of my drink. My rings clink against the porcelain of the cup as I palm it between the bend in my knees, my mood stone shining with a soft pink and purple. Colors I now only associate with Rhys. I don't know why he comes here almost every day to sit with me, but it's a part of my day I look forward to. We don't talk all that much here, but the silence is welcome. It's just nice having someone to sit in silence with. Someone who doesn't pressure me into talking about Nana or question why I spend so much time sitting on top of her gravesite.

"Well, you would know all about being weird, wouldn't you?"

I roll my eyes at his late retort, my eyes skirting over his black university hoodie, over the necklaces resting just below the collar, and up to the hoops adorning the length of his ear. It doesn't matter what the weather is like, rain or sunshine, he is always in some type of hoodie or jacket. Most often, both. He uses his dark clothing and broody expressions as armor in the same way I use memories to keep the nightmares of my past at bay. It's obvious to everyone, including ourselves, that it's all for show. Fuck if you'll find us openly admitting it though.

My eyes find his staring back at me, probably waiting for me to respond. When it becomes obvious that I'm not going to, he brings a knee up to rest his arm over, veins running along his thick forearm earning most of my attention as his eyes flicker toward the darkening sky. "Your roots are showing."

My fingernails tap along my cup, my head leaning against the tombstone like before as I raise a brow at his profile. Although rude, he's not wrong. I do need to redo my hair. My black roots stick out like a sore thumb against the bright platinum strands that hang just above my shoulders. It used to be shiny and long; so long I would accidentally sit on it or shut it in doors. It was strong and healthy, would shine in the light and slide through my fingers without ever having a single tangle. But it's not long anymore, nor is it shiny. A three-a.m. mental breakdown, a pair of kitchen scissors, and two boxes of drugstore bleach is to thank for my hair transformation. I've never been attached to my hair though. Hair is hair. It grows back, so who cares.

"You always know exactly what to say to make a girl swoon, Rhys Elliot." I see the slight twitch of his lips before he catches it, his face turning my way. His long fingers push away the chunk of white-blond hair that falls over his brow before reaching out to grip the short, chopped ends of mine. He tugs hard enough my head slides on the stone it's resting against, roots burning as my face falls closer to his. His hand retreats, pulling strands out with it that hang from his fingers before slipping into the dirt between us.

"You should change it. Dye it purple or something cool." My teeth scrape along my bottom lip as he gives me his profile, his eyes watching me from the corner. "And stop copying me, it makes you look pathetic."

I've learned to look past his insults and rude remarks. I know they're only an attempt to keep people away. Of the few things I've learned about Rhys, I know he wasn't loved properly. He follows almost every compliment with an insult, hides any vulnerability behind bitter words and facial expressions. A product of a broken home and an abusive daddy, Rhys only sees sweet words and soft touches as an act of war. When kindness is only ever given to you as a way to manipulate, you learn to resent it. Something I understand all too well, unfortunately. In the same way that I seek out attention, sweet or painful, Rhys avoids it. After spending time with him, I don't think it's because he doesn't actually want it, because he never is lacking when it comes to his many followers, but because he's scared. Scared to let people get close to him, too scared to trust that he won't be used in the long run.

"It's tragic, really." His eyes narrow at my voice, but he doesn't look directly at me as I speak. "Your hair choice, that is. You have so much potential with the whole dark-and-broody bit you got going on, but that hair? Blond boys just don't do it for me."

I bite the inside of my cheek with his small huff of a laugh, setting my cup off to the side without looking. Rhys tilts his face toward mine once more, the smirk on his lips daring me not to smile with him. I don't. "It's funny you mention it, because I was just thinking the same thing about you." His fingers find their way back to my hair, scraping along the side of my head as he fists it in his palm. His touch is always rough with me; bruising and harsh. "Good thing neither one of us are natural blonds, huh?"

For a fleeting moment, I almost think he's going to kiss me, his lips hovering so near to mine, his grip burning against my scalp. The pain he inflicts is nothing but foreplay for my twisted little mind and I shamelessly lust for it. When he's close like this, I can see those demons he tries to hide, their inky fingers coaxing my own to the surface. Instead, Rhys releases me, pushing away from me like he can't stand touching me even a moment longer. Like he doesn't know if he wants me or wants me dead.

We could be destructive, he and I.

Two beautifully tarnished souls making all the wrong, icky parts of the world just a tiny bit darker with our hearts of tar. The world is a cruel, nasty game of poker, and we were given the shittiest of hands. Tragedies you can't look away from, there's no question we were molded by the devil himself to be the broken bitter carcasses we've become. And like the tragedies we are, we continue to walk our paths of sorrow, live in our misery over and over again, unable to break the cycle of hurt. Like puppies that have been kicked one too many times, we've grown untrusting and wary, even from the things we know could save us.

I'd like to think I could save Rhys; that I could be his dark knight on my skeleton steed. As much as I love his shadows, I wonder what it would be like to be the one he falls into the dark with. What it would be like for him to be the one I fall into.

Sometimes, I think he wonders the same thing.

My arm snapping across my body, I grip the front of his hoodie, one of my fingers unintentionally looping into one of the chains hanging around his neck. It cuts into my skin as I squeeze my fist, and I use the slight bite of pain to spur my bravery. His eyes narrow on my face, his hand wrapping around my wrist like he's going to throw my touch away. He sees something in my expression that makes him pause, and I rush his lips, sinking my teeth into his lower lip and jaw. He hisses into my mouth, the grip on my wrist becoming painful. My tongue swipes out to lap at the sting, sucking in the exhale he blows from his lungs.

My lips close around his for just a whisper of something sweeter, kinder, before I pull back. I know I've pushed my limits by lingering as long as I have already. Wicked little stolen kisses are all he ever lets me get away with. Cruel, angry kisses that spur my heart into a frenzy and coax my blood to rush below my skin.

His lips brush along mine when he speaks, my hand shaking painfully against his chest as his fingers squeeze even tighter. "I doubt your nana would approve of you looking for handouts over her grave."

"You don't know anything about my nana." My skin pebbles as his tongue runs over the divot in his lip that my teeth created. Even if Nana did care, it's not like it would matter. She's dead.

His hand throws my wrist away as he stands, my body falling forward so I have to catch myself with a forearm in the dirt. I look up to find his cruel gaze scorching holes into my flesh.

"And you don't know anything about me." He scoffs at my remark, making me feel almost silly for saying it.

Like always, he leaves me with just a taste, then promptly pushes me away, guarding that black heart of his. He is a tease without even intending to be. It does nothing but make me want him more. Despite how much I want to, I won't allow myself to beg him to stay. I'd rather die than let him see that kind of weakness from me. Something tells me that he'd hate that even more, though.

Sitting up under his gaze, I grab my thermos and take a drink. Putting the lid back on, I see the dark blotches covering my wrist, Rhys's fingers branded into my pale skin. When I look at him, he's looking at my wrist too, lips parted at the sight. Before I can comment, he's spinning away from me. The heat burning behind his blues engrave into my memory as I watch his back disappear from me. My fingers dig into the dirt where he was sitting, my eyes falling to his discarded cup.

"Guess it's just you and me now, Nana."

FIVE
butterfly kisses

She's drunk. And not the cute, giggly kind that I'm usually drawn to, but the sloppy, fall on your face type. To say that puts a dent in my night is a wild understatement. Tonight was supposed to be about us, me and my *Callophrys rubi*. She's been a hard one to snag, but even with this latest hindrance, she's worth it. I watch as she comes stumbling over to where I'm sitting, practically falling into my lap as she comes to a stop. She ditched her heels an hour ago, her feet now dirty from stomping around without them. My hands gripping her upper arms are the only reason she doesn't fall onto the floor.

She's a fucking mess.

"Just... just one more dance. And then we can go to my place." She grins up at me, the minty-sage hue of her eyes settling the annoyance tightening my limbs. She has the most beautiful eyes, my butterfly. Bright green just like a Hairstreak's wings. I knew she would make such a stunning addition to my collection the moment I saw them.

Removing a hand from her arm, I use my fingertips to push some hair away that has fallen into her face. The soft brown is so lackluster compared to those eyes of hers. Shame. "One dance." I return her goofy little smile with one a little less ridiculous, keeping her in place while I swipe my glass of water from the table. "Drink this first."

She rolls her eyes, but doesn't argue, her hand sloppily taking the glass. I try to keep my face neutral as I watch her spill half of the fucking glass down her chin, taking a deep breath through my nose. I've spent far too many fucking nights planning this to have to wait any longer. Priming my butterfly for this took longer than anticipated, and I'm growing dangerously low on patience. She tries to set the glass down before it's gone and I grab the bottom of it, forcing her to finish. She sputters a bit, but eventually swallows it back. Taking it from her hand, I wipe my palm over her chin, slicking away some of the water that missed her mouth.

Nodding toward the dance floor and the other girls she's made drunken friends with, I curl my fingers into my wet palm. "Go."

She drops a messy kiss onto my cheek, missing my mouth, then stumbles away. Fucking ridiculous. I should have known better than to let her drink tonight. I've seen how she gets; it's how she was when I first spotted her. Fucking train wreck of a woman. But not for too much longer.

Soon, very soon, she'll be as flawless as the rest. I wipe my hands off on my thighs, ridding them of the water my butterfly left behind. Resting them there, my thumb swipes over the frayed edge of one of the rips in the fabric, using the rough feel of it to keep myself levelheaded as my butterfly flaps recklessly around the room.

I can hear the song nearing its end and I lean over to scoop up her discarded heels, standing and walking into the mess of bodies toward my *Callophrys rubi*. Her new friends see me before she does, one grabbing her arm with a pouting look on her face. My eyes narrow on her fingers, teeth grinding as the piece of shit woman dares to touch something as precious as my butterfly with her filthy hands.

"Can't she stay? We've just found each other!"

Sage eyes collide with my gaze, her hand softly pushing away the other woman with a shake of her head. She falls into me, wrapping her arms around my waist with another smile. The action is the only thing that saves that vile woman from the anger making my hands shake. Even so, my butterfly's skin feels tainted and dirty. The nagging in the back of my brain wants me to deviate from the plan and take care of this new woman, use the pointed heel of the shoe in my hand to shred her carotid artery right here on the dance floor.

"Can you take me home now?" I realize we're still standing there, my eyes leaving the woman I didn't even notice I was staring at to look down at my butterfly. This close, she looks slightly better than before she drank water, but still not great. Fuck, I need to get her home before she does something stupid like passes out.

I'd fucking lose it.

Forcing my feet to move, I take her hand and start to lead her toward the exit. My sneaker steps in something wet on our way, and I grind my teeth once more. She's fucking barefoot still, getting even more filthy and disgusting. Startling her, I yank her over to a vacant chair and make her sit. "Can you walk in your heels? The ground is dirty."

She shrugs, looking down at her feet like they might have the answer. Breathing through my nose, I rub the side of my head with my knuckles. It's fine. This night isn't ruined. We just need to get to her place and I'll handle it. *It's fine.* Crouching down, I untie my sneakers, ripping them off one at a time to slip onto her feet. I'll be fine in my socks, and although she looks fucking ridiculous, she won't get any dirtier now.

Grabbing her hand, I pull her to a standing position; her smile making me pause. "You're so sweet to me."

I lightly squeeze her fingers instead of responding, moving us back to the exit. I'm not sweet, I'm selfish.

She almost falls onto the floor while opening her apartment door, but I catch her arm, shaking my head at the back of hers. Thank fuck, she lives on the ground level. I would have completely lost all control having to watch her clamber up a set of stairs. Pushing her farther into the space, I step behind her and shut the door. I close my eyes instead of watching her practically fall out of my sneakers, shoving my hands into my jeans' pockets to hide the tremble of irritation.

This night is redeemable. I just need to calm down.

I open my eyes at the feel of her hands on my forearms, her beautiful gaze swallowing me up to cool the anger that was trying to take over. My butterfly smiles up at me, her slender arms circling my waist. I can tell she's going to try to kiss me, so I grab her face in my palms, stopping the progression of her lips. I don't want to kiss her while she's still so filthy.

"Why don't you take a bath?"

She laughs, a confused smile on her face when she realizes I'm not kidding. "Really? A bath?"

I nod, shifting out of her arms as I move her toward the bathroom. She watches me as I push her pink seashell shower curtain to the side and crouch to turn on the tub faucet. I raise a brow at her until she rolls her eyes and shrugs out of the thin straps of her dress. She's leaning a little farther than necessary as she steps from the fabric and I reach out, grabbing her leg just below the knee to make sure she doesn't topple over. If she breaks her neck before I can, I... I don't know what I'd do, but it wouldn't be good for anyone within a five-block radius.

Shutting the water off with one hand, I stand, looking down at my butterfly as she rubs her arms. "It's cold." She's smiling again—always so happy, my butterfly.

"Get in." Leaning against her vanity, I watch her test the water with her palm, hurriedly getting in when it proves to be fine. I reach over and grab

74

her pink loofah, pump some of her bodywash onto it and hand it to her. Smirking, she takes it, rubbing it along her arm at a snail's pace. Breathing through my nose again, I drop to my knees and take it from her. She giggles at me, leaning her head back to relax against the lip of the tub as I run the soap along her body.

It's taken me two months to get my butterfly so trusting, almost two and a half, actually. I almost gave up on her around the third week, but something kept calling me back to her, those minty-sage eyes of hers taunting me in my dreams. She's far too beautiful to be allowed to run amuck like she's been doing. No, she belongs pinned to my wall, strung up and admired. After some persistence, her weak little walls fell, and I slipped into her life seamlessly. I was the poisonous fruit she couldn't resist biting, her naughty secret that she kept hidden from her other friends or family. Unknowingly, she made that part incredibly easy for me. We only went to parts of town where we wouldn't be seen. I wasn't ever introduced to anyone she associates with. From any one of her friends' and family's perspective, I don't exist.

Dropping her soapy loofah into the water, I slide my hand up along the inside of her leg, my heart picking up its pace. My *Callophrys rubi* knows she belongs in my collection, even if only subconsciously. Her legs shift in the water, the pink of her lips titling in a small smile as my palm presses along her wet skin. She set up everything for me so perfectly that we were clearly meant to be. My fingers skim past her belly button as one of her wet arms rises to grip the back of my nape. Water drips down the front of my shirt and splats onto the tile near my knees.

My fingers find the dip at the bottom of her throat, letting her pull my face to her lips. She's clean now, her touch no longer feeling contaminated. I suck her tongue past her lips and lap at the sweetness of her mouth. My hands are shaking again, but this time it's not from anger. I almost can't breathe, my other hand moving to cradle her cheek. Pulling my face away from her, I fall into the mint of her eyes. I was right not to give up tonight.

"You're so beautiful, my butterfly."

She smiles at my compliment, her mouth opening with a response I don't let slip out. Her words disappear underneath the rippling of the water's surface, her head pushed under with the part of her lips, round bright eyes shining like diamonds in the sea. There's always a moment of stillness when they go under the water, a moment of confusion and maybe even disbelief. It's important to get a good grip in that split second or risk them getting free. I adjust my hands slightly, shifting my body farther over the tub as she thrashes. Her hands are grabbing at my arms, her nails sinking into them deep enough to draw blood. A knee comes up and knocks into my elbow, almost making me lose my grip, but I press down harder.

I can feel her heart pounding against my fingertips, banging a tune of terror that burrows in my gut. Her eyes haven't closed once, round saucers shimmering the prettiest shade of green below the rippling of the water's surface. It coaxes my blood to boil beneath my skin, the stunning beauty of my butterfly the best aphrodisiac on the planet. My hips press against the side of the tub, her arms slapping up toward my face, jerking me around in the same rhythm of her body. Water is splashing all over the floor, her bare legs shining as they kick the sides of the tub. I can't help but allow myself to give in to the intimacy of it all. My head rolls back as her nails drag along the skin of my arm once again, lips parting on a moan as her heel hooks over the side of the tub.

Her movements are slowing, her limbs looking heavy and weak, but her eyes never close. Those beautiful minty greens stay locked on mine as her arms drop into the water and the last air bubble leaves her parted lips. My fingers unwrap from her, a hand trailing to rub along the slit of her lips as my hips knock into the side of the tub. I press my thumb roughly against her mouth, blood welling up in a small streak I can barely see as the water rocks with the shift of my hips banging it back and forth. Feeling the cusp of my release, I yank my butterfly from the water and press her wet, slack lips to mine. I moan into her mouth as I lick the edge of her teeth, pounding my release into the tub as I breathe air into my butterfly's limp form.

Letting her slip through my grip, I watch her splash back below the surface, my breaths ragged as I stare at the rippling form of my *Callophrys rubi*. Lifting my arms, I see several deep cuts from her nails and drop to my forearms on the edge of the tub. I'm tired, but I have to clean up. No one ever tells you how exhausting it is drowning someone, especially the ones who like to fight.

Forcing myself up, I open a drawer in the vanity and grab out a pair of fingernail clippers. Going back to the tub, I kneel back down and grab one of my butterfly's hands.

I clip each one of her nails down as far as I can, scraping the bits of skin under fingers off as I go. She was able to get a few good scratches in. I want to make sure I leave with no evidence of me being here. Dropping her hand, I grab the other and give it the same treatment. I reach and grab a washrag from the top of her towel rack, going back over her hands with the remaining soap in the tub, making sure to really scrub what's left of her fingernails. Wringing the wet rag into the water, I bunch it into my fist and stand, taking a minute to admire the way my butterfly's hair floats around her face.

It may have been dull before, but it's nothing short of gorgeous now. She's as beautiful as a sea goddess, floating just below the surface with her unblinking green orbs. Walking from the room, I grab the pale-green origami butterfly from underneath a magnet on the fridge and bring it back to the bathroom. I'd made it for her weeks prior, a gift that reminded me every day of what was to come. Kneeling beside her once more, I place the origami butterfly on the edge of the tub next to a small puddle of water. Careful not to knock it into the water, I lift my butterfly's hand once more and place a kiss onto her fingers before lifting the plug in her tub. I observe the water swirl down the drain for a moment, then watch my butterfly's pruned flesh kiss the air as it sinks from her skin.

I don't like to play favorites, but I think tonight's little butterfly might just be. Letting her arm slip back into the retreating water, I stand and leave the room without another glance. My clothes are still wet, but I had left extra here in anticipation of needing them. I go and get them now, replacing their spot in my bag with the wet ones along with the rag. Thankfully, my shoes aren't wet because I didn't pack a spare pair of those. I pause outside the bathroom door, tempted to open it up and take another peek, but I force myself to move, to walk down the hall and put my sneakers back on. With my backpack full of wet clothes, I open the front door and step out into the night.

I'm proud of myself for not letting this night get ruined. That wasn't exactly what I'd had planned, but it was even more beautiful.

Nothing short of utter perfection.

SIX

hadley

It's hot today. Way hotter than the weather forecast called for. My eyes slide to Rhys, peeking at him out of the corner of my eye. If I'm hot in my tee and shorts, he has to be dying in his black jacket and denim. My fingers lightly trail over the late-summer mums as I watch him frown down at his phone, the petals soft beneath my fingertips. "Are you hot?"

He looks up, a mumbled, "No," growled my way as he tucks his phone away to grab a cigarette. Our eyes briefly meet as he lights it, my attention turning back to the flowers. There are a few butterflies fluttering along the blooms, their dusty yellow wings glinting in the waning sunlight. I hold my hand between the flowers, coaxing one onto my fingers. Smoke blows along my cheek as Rhys moves closer, the stink of it stinging my nostrils as he asks, "What're you doing?"

I can hear the amusement in his voice, but there's no smile on his lips when I give him a quick glance. It's such a bad habit, smoking, but what isn't these days? I actually like the smell of the smoke, the smell of fresh lit tobacco and alcohol on the breath. It reminds me of the better parts of my childhood, of the sweet neighbor who lived next door from my parents. He may have started drinking at the crack of dawn, but he was kind to me. His liquor made him uncaring and extremely trusting. I remember watching his niece cry at his funeral; big fat tears that slid off her chin to splat onto the top of his coffin. Beautifully heartbreaking. That's what Rhys is too. He smells like cigarettes and coffee—spicy, rich and earthy. He's like a walking, breathing, living version of my favorite scent. It's strange but comforting.

Fluttering wings crawl along my fingers to the back of my hand and I look at Rhys again. He's actually smirking now, his lips wrapping around his cigarette as he watches me.

"Do you like bugs?" I ask. My eyes leave the cobalt of his to watch the butterfly walk across the back of my hand.

"Bugs? Like spiders and shit?" The smoke from his mouth puffs along my lips as he leans in to look at the flapping yellow wings still crawling across my skin. "No. I squish them."

"But you like butterflies." It's not a question. The small tilt of his lips created by the little insect tells me he does, or at least more than other bugs. I roll my hand over, encouraging the little butterfly to settle on my palm.

"Yea, I guess."

"I hate them," I say. Finding his face, my eyes settle back on the twist of his lips. Is it normal to be jealous that his smile is for a bug and not me? "Butterflies are little liars. Master manipulators at making everyone think they're something they're not." I swallow as his tongue wets his lips, watching them close around his smoke before looking back at my hand and the bug stretching its wings there. "They're ugly little caterpillars that have learned to grow pretty wings of deceit." I slap my other hand down, smashing the little yellow butterfly in my palm. Brushing my hands together, I watch it fall to the dirt, yellow dust from its wings staining my fingers. "They're nothing but pretty bugs."

Rhys snorts, his eyes on the butterfly at my feet as he drops his cigarette next to it. His sneaker rubs both into the dirt. "You're so fucking weird."

"You're my butterfly." His eyes find mine, at my confession, his hands tucking into his jacket pockets as he watches me.

"Are you saying I'm a bug? Or that you hate me?"

"Neither." Turning to face him more fully, my sneakers bump against his, my finger rising to trail along the open zipper of his jacket. He watches me as I press along the seam hard enough it scratches my skin. "You're a pretty liar." I press into his zipper even harder, using the pain to spur my confidence. "And just like the butterflies, you've somehow manipulated me to see past all of those secrets you keep." I can feel the blood welling up on the pad of my finger, and I pull my hand away from him to look at the small drops of ruby gathering along the tip.

Rhys snatches my hand, drawing my gaze to his as he presses his thumb into my cut so more blood drips down. "You should be more careful, Hadley. Saying shit like that makes me think you want to join my collection of broken hearts."

I pull our joined hands toward my mouth, licking the blood up the length of my finger, over the rough edge of his fingertips and over my cut as he watches. The coppery tinge brightens my senses as I look into his denim eyes. Despite the way the words dripped venom from his lips, I don't think he'd actually be so opposed to the idea. I'm not above letting his demons paint their runes of destruction over my skin even if all it ever gets me is a night of fake bliss. He can stick me in his jar of hearts for all I care, add me to his collection of sins.

He drops my hand when I'm silent for too long and I look back at the mums. The butterflies have all left, I notice. "My nana used to collect things." I hear his snort at my abrupt change of subject and feel his heat lick along my back as I tear a few petals from the bush and let them slip through my fingers. "Stained glass and wind chimes." Her entire house was covered with her little treasures, stained glass pieces hanging around every window. She even had this special film she'd had installed on her windows, so that every morning her white-and-beige furniture and accents would glow with a rainbow of colors. I know she kept the lighter theme in her house for that reason, so there was always some kind of prism of light shining along the floors and walls. "I hated the wind chimes. Her house was the noisiest one on the block. She had at least a dozen hanging from her porch and there was this stray cat that would come around like clockwork to bang them around every evening. I swear it knew how much it annoyed me and did it on purpose."

Ignoring the yellow and white swirling in my ring, I pluck some more petals. Rhys's breath burns along my ear. "Why didn't you get rid of the cat?"

I shrug, turning my face to peek at him out of the corner of my eye. "My nana liked it and that was reason enough for me to just deal with it."

"Your parents are dead." It's not what I was expecting him to say, but I'm not surprised he brought it up. It wasn't a question either. I've never told him they were dead, but I guess it's not hard to figure out since I never talk about them and only my nana.

"Yes." Dropping the straps on my backpack, I drop it to my feet. Turning around, I sit next to it, raising my knees to rest my cheek against them as Rhys sinks next to me. His fingers brush along my thigh as he gets comfortable, his eyes on my face, waiting for me to say more. "They died in a house fire when I was fifteen. The firefighters who found me said it was a miracle I survived. That I must have had a guardian angel watching over me."

Drip. Drip. Drip.

"Put that down and come here, Hadley," my mother's voice calls from the doorway, the silver butterfly clips holding back the hair at her temples glinting in the light of a candle on the shelf. I ignore her, shaking my head in silent defiance. "Be a good girl and come here."

Drip. Drip. Drip.

92

A good girl. I snort, my lips twisting at my mother. That's not possible; nothing I ever do is good enough for my parents. I am never good enough for them. My eyes land on my father's unblinking gaze from where I stand near his chair. It's a nice change to not hear him slinging around his insults and disappointment at my behavior. That's all he ever fucking does; all he ever has to say to me. I hear the floorboards creak as my mother takes a step into the room and my attention turns back to her. Her hands are shaking despite the confident bite of her tone just moments ago. Is she scared? What the fuck could she possibly be scared for? I'm the one going to be punished, not her. "Why are you trembling?"

Drip. Drip. Drip.

She ignores my question, her eyes flickering between my hand and my face. "Knock this off right now, young lady!" One of her hands is clutching a pleat in her long skirt, the other gripping the doorframe like she needs the support to keep from toppling over.

Drip. Drip. Drip.

The crease in her brow lightens just a bit when I step forward in her direction, then quickly deepens when she realizes I'm not coming to her. My foot steps into something warm and wet when I pass my father's chair, my toes sticking to the floor as I walk to the candle on the shelf. Letting the hammer I was holding slip through my fingers to my feet, I reach for it. The hot glass burns against my palms as I cradle it to my chest, but I don't mind, taking a deep breath to inhale its scent. It smells like sugared donuts, far too pleasant to be in a hellhole like this. I look back at my father, his silent face staring back at me. "No."

I don't know how long I was silent, but Rhys doesn't seem to mind, his legs stretched alongside me as his fingers pick at a tear in his denim. "My parents weren't very nice people, and I don't miss them." His face turns to meet mine and I'm surprised to see nothing but subtle understanding on it. Most people get uncomfortable when I say things like that. They can't possibly understand how I could think that. But I should have already known that Rhys would get it. He's probably the only person who would.

"I don't believe in guardian angels." I watch his jaw work as he turns away from me, staring at the hard edges of his profile. "If they're somehow able to save people from fires and car accidents, then they should also be able to save them from abuse and neglect." He pauses, tongue running over his lips. "But they don't, because they don't exist."

My lips part with a loud breath, my head raising as I drop my legs to lay flat like Rhys's. My sneaker toe accidentally taps against his foot, and he kicks mine back much harder than necessary. "Or maybe, they do exist and people like us just aren't good enough to get one."

He shakes his head, his bright blond hair flopping over his frown. "Doesn't even matter. People like us don't need them." His hand raises, roughly pushing the hair from his face. "We're our own guardian angels. We don't need anyone's help. We'll save ourselves or die trying." His cornflower eyes find mine, scrunched at the edges. "You're strong and your parents were weak. That's why you made it out and they didn't."

His words feel oddly like a compliment, and I can't help the slight purse of my lips in reaction. People don't pay me compliments that don't hold a hidden agenda, but his feels genuine. And that makes me feel *something*.

He looks away from me, ending our silent moment. "How'd your nana die?" His question chills my skin despite the heat.

Now, I'm frowning. The thought of her bringing that familiar gut-wrenching ache. "She fell and hit her head. I found her when I came home from classes one day." I feel Rhys shift beside me, but I don't look, instead I fix my eyes on the sun disappearing over the hill. "She was old. The coroner said she probably died instantly."

"Do you still live in her house? With all the wind chimes?" I shake my head at his question, listening to his lighter flick on as he lights up another cigarette.

"No. The bank took it after she passed. She had a reverse mortgage or some shit." I left everything but a single wind chime when I moved out. The bank tried to contact me several times about getting the rest, but what would I have done with all that stuff? I didn't want it, so I let them deal with it. I'm not sure why I chose the wind chime that I did, but at least hanging it by my window, it doesn't make much noise.

It was lonely after she was gone, just me and her bright rainbow house. Her wind chimes would torment me throughout the day, reminding me of her with every blow of the breeze. I found myself wandering the city a lot then, doing whatever I could to keep myself busy and out of the house.

"Saltwater taffy?"

My eyes shift over to the elderly man seated near my bench, dropping to the handful of wrapped candy sitting in his palm. You're not supposed to take candy from a stranger, but I doubt this old man in a wheelchair is all that wicked. Smiling, I reach out and take a piece of taffy. "Thank you. What kind is it?"

He nods, stuffing the candies back in his pocket after taking a piece for himself. "Watermelon I think. Maybe strawberry?"

He shrugs and I watch as his shaky fingers unwrap his sweet, popping mine into my mouth. I nod when he looks over at me, eating his own. "I think you're right. It tastes like watermelon."

We sit in silence, the sound of our mouths quietly smacking over the sticky candy barely audible over the bustle of the city. After a bit, the man pulls out another, softly nudging my arm with a "take it" gesture.

I smile again, slipping it from his fingers. "Where'd you get it? I haven't had taffy in years."

He snorts, unwrapping another piece for himself. "I stole it from the front desk at the nursing home."

I laugh at that, crumpling my candy wrappers between my fingers. "You're allowed to leave?" I ask, referring to him sitting with me at the bus stop.

"Nope."

I laugh again, my head turning when a loud, "Larry!" is shouted in our direction.

The man, Larry I'm assuming, sighs loudly, eyeing me from under his large unruly brows. "I've been caught."

A nurse comes running up to us, her hands dropping to her knees as she reaches Larry's side with a frown. "Larry! You know you can't just take off like that. You're not going to be allowed to go outside without supervision if you keep disappearing." She looks over at me, smiling for a moment before her eyes fall back onto Larry, "Are those taffies, Larry? You know we need to watch your blood sugar!"

Larry frowns at her, his lips pursing but he says nothing. He reaches into his pocket to grab his candy, holding his hand out to me. "You might as well take it before Hitler here does."

Biting back a smile, I take his offered candy, cradling it in my lap as Larry's nurse grabs onto the handles of his wheelchair. "Thank you."

"That's not very nice Larry," his nurse says as she starts to pull him away.

He rolls his eyes, looking at me as he's rolled backward. "Feel free to come visit me at Rivercrest Retirement Home... bring me something good if you do."

I laugh, nodding as he's turned around. "Maybe I'll do that."

Larry had shown up at just the perfect time for me, when I was in the midst of losing myself after Nana's death. Talking to him had been the first time I'd felt something besides just sad.

Rhys stands abruptly, startling me from my thoughts and I look up at him from the grass, watching the bobbing orange end of his cigarette as he talks around it. "You're a sad, weird girl, Hadley."

I can't help the small laugh that slips out, grabbing my backpack as I stand. Apparently, Rhys has had his fill of talking and emotions for the day. "But you like it."

His eyes narrow on my face as his lips close around his cigarette, his fingers coming up to hold it as he takes a drag. Smoke blows from his nose as he holds my gaze. "I don't like anything about you," he says as he pulls the cigarette from his lips.

I smile at his frown, shifting my backpack onto my back. "See you later, butterfly." I turn away from him, being the first to walk away this time. I feel his gaze on my back but don't look, my fingers digging into the straps of my bag as I walk. I heard what he didn't say, what he never says. Rhys Elliot likes me as much as I like him, whether he's willing to admit it or not.

SEVEN
butterfly kisses

I wasn't expecting this. I came out tonight to see my butterfly and what do I find? My *Celastrina argiolus* blushing behind her napkin over the piece of shit she's on a date with. I almost didn't notice her, all gussied up with her curled hair and red lips. Surely, my butterfly wouldn't be out here with someone else. Not *my* butterfly. But it was her I was looking at through the restaurant window, smiling at some pathetic Wall-Street-looking trash no less.

My eyes have been narrowed on the pale yellow of his button-up since I sat down at my own table to watch them. Every second that ticks by is gasoline thrown onto my inner rage. Every little giggle that slips past her ruby lips, every flutter of her lashes, every little touch. They should all be mine and I have to sit here and watch my butterfly be soiled by this filth. I'll admit that when I first sat down at my table, I was naïve enough to think this might be some kind of friendly exchange, not an actual date. How stupid of me.

"Has someone come to help you yet?"

I jerk my attention from the happy couple to the waitress standing by my table, pen at the ready like she already knows the answer to her question. Grabbing the menu from the table, I hand it out to her, my eyes briefly landing on my butterfly as her fingers pinch around the laminated bifold. "Not yet. Can I get a rare steak and sweet tea?"

She smiles, tucking the menu under her arm as she writes. I might've found her pretty any other night with the dimple in her cheek and the mess of coppery hair piled on top of her head. Unfortunately for her, or rather fortunately, I have my hands full with my naughty butterfly tonight. "Sure thing. Do you want any sides? Or just the steak tonight?"

"Just the steak."

She says something but my attention is already across the room, so I don't hear it. I doubt my butterfly realizes that everyone can see her dates hand rubbing along her thigh beneath the table, or that when she uncrosses her legs, her navy-blue panties flash the entire fucking room. All of her attention is on the prick she's with. They seem far more familiar than I care to admit, like this isn't the first date they've been on. I hate it. I hate how happy my butterfly looks. I hate how she's oblivious to everything but him. She hasn't once looked my way, never even felt my presence.

It's annoying and insulting.

I almost stand up; my hands trembling with rage as they grip the edge of the table, the tablecloth wrinkling in my palms, but my waitress sneaks up on me to set a glass of water in front of me. Forcing myself to sit back in my chair once more, I thank her retreating back. Despite how much it kills me to see my butterfly flap her wings for someone else, I can't do anything about it. Not yet. Not here. I wasn't planning on adding *Celastrina argiolus* to my collection just yet. I wanted to spend more time with her first, but she's made the decision for me with this little escapade of hers.

Light blue. She was wearing a soft light blue cotton dress when I first saw her, reading a book in the middle of the bread isle. She'd smiled when I'd caught her, laughed when I commented. Her blue dress had twirled, floated on a breeze like a Holly Blue's wings, when she spun to leave after giving me her number written on the back of a faded bookmark.

UNSETTLED

She can pretend she's not mine all she wants, but she can't hide from the facts any longer.

My eyes barely leave them as my steak and utensils are placed in front of me, my lips twisting into a fake smile for the waitress. I nod in acknowledgment to whatever she says, my hand closing around the napkin holding my silverware. Shaking it out, I peel my eyes from the disaster playing out before me and grab the steak knife. Shifting a wary glance around the room, I use the knife to tear my napkin, using my hands to rip it the rest of the way when it catches so that I have two separate pieces. Tucking one of the pieces into my jacket pocket, I tear the remaining piece in half again so that I have two squares. I shove one of the fabric squares into my pocket with the other, my eyes finding my butterfly as I fold the remaining square into a butterfly.

It's an ugly pale cream with ripped, frayed edges; nothing but garbage compared to the one I would have made her if she hadn't decided to up our timeline. I hate it, but not nearly as much as I hate my butterfly's date. I watch as they both stand from their table, my eyes burning when their fingers link while walking toward the exit. Standing up shortly after them, I reach into my denim pocket to toss cash onto the table, watching the back of my butterfly's head as they walk out the door. I didn't touch my steak, but I didn't actually want it. I snatch the steak knife from the table before I leave, tucking it away inside of my jacket as I make my way out of the restaurant. Stepping onto the sidewalk, I pause, unsure where they went.

Lucky for me, they aren't too far ahead, my butterfly's laugh drifting over all the other noises, drawing my eyes their way. Such a great time she's having. Such a wonderful night for them both.

I can't fucking stand it.

I feel like I've been cheated of my prize. I have a specific way I like to do things, a way that ensures I get my butterfly in perfect condition for my collection. This is not fucking it. Each step I take is slightly faster than the last, my heart thumping against my ribs in an angry rhythm. All I can see is my butterfly, and the sight isn't nearly as sweet as it should be.

Just seeing the way her cheeks turn pink when her date leans to whisper in her ear has me fighting the urge to push my way through the crowd to yank her from him. The fact that she actually looks happy, that she sounds happy, grates on my nerves like nothing else. There's a nagging in the back of my skull that tells me it might not just be because she's my fucking butterfly; that maybe the twisting in my gut might be closer to jealousy than rage. Shoving my hands into my jacket pockets, my fingers wrap around the handle of the steak knife, effectively cooling my racing mind. No. I'm not jealous, that's impossible. I don't care about frivolous nonsense like relationships. At least that's what I tell myself as the pit in my stomach grows, watching my butterfly flutter in front of me.

They're getting farther from the main foot traffic, making it harder for me to use the passing bodies as coverage. The more I take in our surroundings and my attention off of my butterfly, I realize we are actually going in the direction of the college bars. Of course, this trash goes to the same school as my butterfly. It makes sense now why they're so familiar with each other. They probably have some of the same classes, maybe even share the same dorm. How cute of them, turning their pathetic little lives into some kind of romance novel. Rom-com no doubt because this fucker is nothing but a joke.

I look away from them, eyes dropping to the old brick road we're walking along. It circles the outskirts of the campus, red brick worn down by time that adds a certain charm to the place I've always liked. I'm lucky that it's the weekend and this area gets busy; that and the cloak of night hiding me are the only things preventing me from sticking out like a sore thumb. I have no fucking plan for this, and I always have a plan. I always know what I'm going to do weeks in advance. I should just let it go, force myself to go home and stick to the plan. But I know I can't do that. I wouldn't be able to. The thought of her betrayal would plague my every waking thought just as it's doing now and poison our connection.

I look up just in time to see my butterfly hurry into an alleyway, pulled by her frat boy in a giggling huff. I don't have to be a genius to know why they're sneaking off. That douche hasn't been able to keep his hands off of my butterfly all night. He probably couldn't wait a second longer to taste what's mine. I already know my butterfly tastes as sweet as honey and her skin is softer than Egyptian silk. She's beautiful with her tanned skin and chocolate eyes. She's a ruby in a bin full of emeralds, rich and warm. Like all the rest before her, I knew she was meant to be mine the second I saw her. My beautiful *Celastrina argiolus* fluttering her wings, begging to be one of my treasures.

I slowly pass the alleyway they went down, turning my face to find them almost hidden from sight. If I wasn't specifically looking, I wouldn't have seen them halfway down it and engulfed in the shadows. I pause, leaning my back against the building behind me while pulling my phone from my back pocket. I pretend to text as a group of people pass, quickly glancing to make sure no one is looking before diving into the darkness myself.

Tucking my phone away, my fingers find the handle of my knife once more. My sneakers are almost silent on the pavement under my feet, my eyes blinking to adjust to the darkness as I creep toward the hushed tones further down the alley. I almost can't hear them over the pounding in my ears, my heart losing it when I realize I'm not hearing whispers, but soft moans. My fingers tighten painfully on the handle in my hand, pulling it from my pocket as I move to silently stand behind the man rubbing the dust from my butterfly.

With angry, trembling fingers, I slam my knife into the side of his neck. His filthy hands leave my butterfly, slapping uselessly at his throat while I pull it out and shove him out of my way. My butterfly doesn't even see me, her hands reaching for him in confusion. They really chose the best spot for this, because it's so dark she can't even tell what's going on less than a foot from her face. Reaching forward, I grip her soft curls and yank her away from the man she's trying to speak to. A short, startled scream escapes her kiss-swollen lips, but I quickly silence it by smacking her head against the building behind her while releasing her hair.

Poor thing is so confused she's not even fighting me, barely even aware of me, it would seem, as her arms raise to cradle her bleeding head. The man at my feet is still gurgling but otherwise disposed. This feels rather uneventful after all that angry buildup and that makes me even angrier. How dare he tarnish my butterfly and then give up so easily. How dare she allow such a pathetic waste of human to stroke her wings. My arm snaps out to grip her cheeks in my palm, squeezing as hard as I can while making her look at me.

It's so dark I can't see the color of her eyes, but I know the chocolate is melting, can feel her tears running along my fingers. I can vaguely see her blinking up at me, small whimpers leaving her pinched lips. She's not even fighting me, just crying. "I'm disappointed in you."

A light flicks on in an above window, casting a low dim light just enough to let her make out my features. We are both blinking to adjust to the change, her hands latching onto me with recognition, nails scraping against the material of my jacket as she finally gives me some kind of reaction that isn't pathetic. "What the fuck is wrong with you? What did you do to Daniel? Daniel! Dan—"

I bash her head back against the building once again, effectively silencing her once more. Her hands try to yank my arm down, but I don't budge. I've done this so many fucking times, her weak little arms aren't going to move mine anytime soon. "None of that now."

I smash her head once more when she starts to wiggle again, small whimpers leaving her lips. Her body sags just a bit like she's getting close to losing consciousness, and I lightly shake her face. "Did you know that butterflies have scales on their wings?" I shake her head in my palm, answering my question for her as she blinks at me, her knees trying to buckle. "Well, they do. And do you know what happens when people touch their wings?" I shake her head again, tutting at her. "You're kind of stupid, do you know that?" I make her nod, smiling to myself. "Their scales get wiped away when you touch them. Their already thin wings become weakened and more prone to tears and damage. Just like yours are now."

I can tell she's about to pass out on me, her eyes barely open now. Fucking pathetic. She'll be added to my collection like the rest, but her box will be shrouded with disappointment. She had so much fucking potential. I angrily slam my steak knife into her gut, her droopy eyes suddenly wide awake with shock as her mouth creates a perfect "O". I drag it up to the bottom of her rib cage then step back, pulling it with me. She slides down the building at her back, arms aimlessly clutching at her waist as she drops to the ground.

Looking at her tangled with her douche lover isn't the ending I wanted, and I angrily toss my makeshift napkin butterfly onto their limp bodies. How fucking disappointing. Taking one of the spare napkin pieces from my pocket, I scrub the knife's handle down before throwing it farther down the alley to mix with all the other trash.

UNSETTLED

Looking down at myself, I can't even see if I have blood on me or not. Good thing it's dark. I'll just have to avoid the lighted areas on my way home, I guess. I'm wearing dark denim and a black jacket, or this may have been an issue. It's just a reminder that I didn't plan this, and I feel myself getting annoyed all over again.

Eyes dropping to my butterfly, I shake my head. For the first time in a very long time, I don't feel even the tiniest bit satisfied with the bloodshed. Walking to the end of the alley toward the main road, I listen for anyone walking my way before stepping out onto the sidewalk. I won't let this happen again. I won't let myself feel this again, but that doesn't help me right fucking now. Hidden in my pockets, my hands won't stop shaking. My heart is still angrily pounding against my ribs, waiting for the grand finale that won't happen. I can't leave myself like this without risking having a complete fucking blowout.

My shoulder bumps against someone as I turn the corner, but I don't bother to apologize. I'm not sorry. If anything, I wish I'd pushed them hard enough to get struck by oncoming traffic. Seeing their face stuck to the grill might have helped settle my racing lungs. I need fucking *something* to quell the manic need to feel satisfied. I need *someone*. But not just anyone, I need someone who can handle my very specific set of needs for the night, and the more I think about it, I think I have the perfect little weirdo for the job.

EIGHT

hadley

I'm sitting on a pillow in my bay window seat, staring out into the black woods behind my house when I hear the front door open. I already know who it is, so I don't look. An hour ago, I got a random phone call asking for my address from a very familiar voice. It would be an understatement to say I was surprised. He sounded rougher than usual, off. The urgency that leaked through the conversation told me he needed me, and the desperate pathetic part of me loved that.

Turning my face from the window, I watch as Rhys steps into my small living area. His hair is damp as if he showered recently, wet strands hanging over his brow as he shucks his jacket off of his big shoulders to fall onto the floor. I can feel his eyes piercing into my skin, his gaze unwavering as he silently reaches behind his back to rip the hoodie he's wearing over his head. It drops to the floor with his jacket. It's almost strange seeing him without either, my lips parting as he loses his shirt next. I don't know how I was expecting things to go, but I'm not mad about where we're ending up. If anything, I'm nervous.

He toes off his sneakers as he walks toward me, the hard, flat expanse of his chest begging for most of my attention. His muscles ripple in the dimmed lighting of my loft, all of his dips and edges highlighted by the shadows. Shifting so that my feet find the floor, I face him head-on, my eyes blinking at the sting when his hand finds the hair at the back of my head to jerk me to stand before him.

"I don't have time for your weird nonsense tonight, Hadley, so listen carefully." I swallow as his breath hits my lips, my pulse pounding against the press of his thumb as his other hand grips my jaw. "I'm going to fuck you until you're crying for me to stop, begging me to leave you alone." The hand in my hair tightens, pulling the hair at my scalp painfully but I don't blink or give him any indication that his touch affects me. "Whether you want it or not, I don't care. In fact, I hope you don't."

My mouth opens before I can stop it, shameless words spilling from my lips. Those demons of his are swirling just below the surface and I can't help myself from trying to get them out. "Promises, promises. Don't get my hopes up if you don't intend to keep your word." It's false bravado I'm spitting, but not a lie. Fuck, I want that. I want nothing more than to feel every ounce of pain this brutal man has to offer. I don't know what has him so wound up, so bent on destruction, but I'm fucking here for it.

He smiles, a full-blown, toothy grin that has my gut clenching with anxious energy. It's absolutely stunning and nothing short of terrifying. My head is tilted further back for him by the hand in my hair, a small almost inaudible gasp falling from my mouth at the bite of pain. His tongue reaches out to lap at the part of my lips, dipping to taste the space between my teeth. I want to touch him, feel the warmth of his skin against my palms, but it almost feels like I need permission. My fingers have a light tremble as I risk it, the tips of my nails making little divots in his skin as I press them to his chest.

I suck in the breath he lets out at the contact and swallow it down as his teeth turn vicious on my lips. I can already taste the coppery tinge of my blood, the bruising grip of his fingers on my face, telling what's in store for me. His hands leave my head to grab at the front of my cotton tee. He fists my tits, painfully squeezing them in his palms as his teeth scrape down the column of my throat. My head falls back, the pain he's inflicting, lusting up my wicked mind.

"Take it off. Take everything off."

It's growled into my skin as his teeth continue to brand me. His fingers have found my nipples, yanking at their tight peaks ruthlessly as I try to do what he's commanded, his hands angrily slapping mine away when I take too long. He rips the shirt over my head, and it disappears across the room, followed by my bra that is practically ripped from my skin. My breath is knocked out of me as he shoves me onto the floor unexpectedly, my elbows banging painfully against the carpet as I catch myself. My chest is heaving under his gaze, the cornflower blue of his eyes almost black as he stares down at me. I should feel scared, or at the very least worried, but I don't. Not if the dark pink swirling in my mood stone indicates anything. The shadows are where I always feel the most comfortable, and right now, Rhys is nothing but dark.

He drops to his knees before me and they thud between the part of my legs, loud and hard. Silently, he grips the top of my leggings, fingers scratching the skin of my lower belly as he jerks them down. I lift my hips to help him, watching the slight tremble of his hands as they work the fabric down my legs. I don't think the tremble is his nerves getting the best of him. I think he's holding back, keeping whatever monster he's hiding, behind his navy blues at bay. My leggings disappear like my shirt and bra, and Rhys's eyes narrow on my thighs. Although he could be glaring down at the only clothing remaining on my body, I think his eyes are fixed on something else.

I almost forgot where we were, that I had the lights on, because I let myself get lost in his magnetism. I try to close my thighs, hide the jagged scars lining my skin like thick white lightning bolts, but he grabs my knees, stopping me. One of his rough palms slides down from my knee, his thumb bumping along the ridges of white. His eyes find mine. "Why?"

His hands aren't shaking anymore, I notice, like seeing the slices of hate in my skin has tempered whatever beast he was keeping confined. I swallow as he stares me down, waiting for an answer. I don't like talking about my scars, much less letting people see them. It's no surprise to anyone that I'm a fucking wreck of a human being, but my scars are just that, mine. They're the only marks on my body I've willingly made with my own hand, carved into my flesh with an aching heart and sad mind, trying to feel something that was purely mine. When I mark my flesh, I'm the one controlling my emotions. I'm the one doling out my punishments or rewards. It's one of the few moments I feel even remotely in control. I don't need my ring to tell me how I feel. For a brief moment in time, I just know. "Because the pain is the only thing I'm sure of."

Something resembling understanding purses his lips as a hand slides even higher, his thumb pressing along the seam of my slit through the fabric of my panties. If he was surprised to find the wet spot soaked through, he doesn't act like it. Instead, he reaches behind his back with his free hand, reaching into his back pocket to bring forward a pocketknife. My heart thumps against my ribs as he flicks his wrist, a short, curved blade glinting in the light from the lamp as he holds it above me.

"You going to gut me, butterfly? Flay me like a fish?"

His thumb moves upward, making my breath catch in my chest as he presses ruthlessly on my clit. He leans over me, the warmth of his chest brushing along my aching nipples. I arch into his touch, desperate for more even as his knife disappears. His teeth scratch over my chin, his breath meeting my lip. "Not a single word." His lips close over mine, the touch achingly sweet compared to his usual bite and I practically moan, my lips chasing his when he pulls away to sit back up. "Not a single sound." His thumb dips to my slit, rubbing the wetness through my panties. "Nothing but silence."

He raises the knife, showing it off by turning it side to side in the light. His eyes aren't on my face, but on my chest, trailing their gaze to my stomach, then further down to settle on my pussy. The knife is cold when he places the flat side of its wicked curve on my hot skin, my skin puckering with anxious goosebumps as he makes it follow the same path as his eyes. I feel the fabric of my panties split, the cold tip of the knife sliding just inside the wet lips of my pussy. I gasp at the feel of it, my thighs involuntarily trying to close but catching on Rhys's hips.

He smirks at my reaction, looming over me as he brings the curved blade under the base of my chin. "Not a single sound, Hadley." It's a wicked reminder that's immediately put to the test when his long fingers dip into my slit through the torn fabric of my panties, spreading my pussy lips. His hand with the knife retreats from my throat, the tip lightly scratching a soft pink line as he drags it down my skin. His fingers tease my entrance, not going nearly deep enough to satisfy the aching in my gut, my own slick dripping from his fingers to slide down the crease of my ass.

Shifting my hips in an attempt to get his fingers deeper, the knife on my collarbone is pressed harder into my skin and my palm slaps over my mouth to stop the sound that was about to come out. Rhys's deep chuckle hits me right in the pussy and has it clenching at his fingers as they dip just inside before running along my lips once more. There's a small line of blood trailing from my collarbone, dripping down to the valley between my breasts and I watch Rhys's chest pick up as he follows its path with his eyes. His pupils are blown when they meet mine, the sight of my blood taking his arousal to another level of wicked.

The knife trails lower, circling one of my nipples and his hand withdraws from my pussy. My hips chase his fingers, watching as he unbuttons his denim, my eyes fixed on the long, hard erection he withdraws from the confines of his pants. The tip is shiny with precum, and I find myself sitting forward, my hand reaching to grab him in my palm. He stops me, the tip of his knife digging into the weight of my left tit. "New rule, no moving."

My mouth opens to argue, fingers still stretched toward his skin, but he slices a thin jagged line down my ribcage in warning. Not hard enough to draw blood, but enough to leave a stinging pink scratch. Closing my mouth, I lie back onto the carpet, my fingers digging into the soft shag to keep myself from reaching for him again. His teeth flash at the frown dipping my lips but he doesn't comment on my sudden change of tune.

The silver blade reflects off the lamp across the room as he lifts it to my other breast, giving it the same torturous tease as he had the other before slowly dragging it down toward my belly button. My eyes close as his fingers find my soaking pussy once more, his long digits swiping from the bottom of my ass to my clit to scoop up my slick. Opening my eyes at the loss of his touch, I meet his dark gaze just as he sticks his fingers into his mouth, sucking them clean with a low groan deep in this throat. The sound alone has my hips shifting in front of him, silently begging him to stop with the slow teasing.

He shakes his head at me, flicking his wrist so quickly I don't see the line he's cut into my skin until the blood starts to well up in tiny little droplets. I bite my bottom lip to keep from making any noise, the slight bit of pain jumbling with the throbbing between my legs to muddle my brain. His tongue lands hot on my skin, lapping along the cut in a way that has my body trembling to fight the urge to arch into him. Almost in the same breath, I feel his dick bob along my slit, just the tip breaching my inner lips to tease me further. Sitting up from me, he pulls out before slamming back into me. It effectively cuts off the protest that was about to slip from my lips and slides my back along the carpet with a force that covers my back in rug burn. He either forgot the significance of him fucking me raw, even knowing my extensive background of partners, or he is just simply uncaring.

I moan against my will, my head rolling back into the carpet as he grips my hip with one hand and slices the knife across my skin with the other. The grip on my hip bone is painfully bruising and his thrusts vicious; almost too hard, too rough, ramming into me in a way that makes my pussy sting with each violent slap of his balls. Another moan slips out and I smack my hand back over my mouth, the sound earning me yet another slice. Despite ruthlessly pounding between my legs, Rhys is following the same path as his blade, licking up the blood that leaks from the spots that sink just a tad too deep. Little sounds keep leaking through my fingers and each one is followed by another nick or slice. It's a mixture of soft and punishing that has me quickly feeling the tightening in my gut of an impending orgasm.

My skin is hot and sweaty, and I can feel the short strands of my hair sticking to my face as I rock my head back and forth with pinched eyes to keep from screaming through my fingers. Each thrust of Rhys's hips is painful on both the friction burn on my back and my pussy; my body stinging from various slices covering my body, an all-over burn that does nothing but cause more slick to seep down my ass cheeks onto the carpet. My orgasm hits me hard and fast, a shaking moan slipping from my chest as Rhys's mouth locks onto one of my tits, his teeth sinking into the plump flesh as his tongue flicks the nipple. It hurts so fucking good that I can't stop my thighs from closing tighter around his waist, uncaring of the slice that tracks across my hip for it.

My body sags in defeat, my hand slipping away from my mouth to land next to my face as Rhys continues his delicious abuse. I watch him as he rams into me, my slick easing some of the burn as he drives hard and fast to reach his own release. His hair is dry now but for a few pieces sticking to his forehead with sweat. His muscles flex as he pumps. The denim on his hips has slipped even lower, hanging around his thick thighs. He's stunning in all his angry glory, his lips twisted into a nasty scowl even as I feel thick spurts of his cum spray my gut.

He's out of breath, his hips finally stilling as he admires the mess he's made of my skin. Letting the knife slip from his fingers, he runs both of his hands up my ribcage, small blots of blood spreading along with them as he presses into my cuts. I hiss through my teeth when his fingers find the deep bite mark on my breast, the skin already bruising an ugly shade of purple and green. He ignores it, continuing his exploration of his handy work until he reaches my face, one hand gripping my jaw and drops himself onto a forearm to loom over me. Without a word, he kisses my lips, soft and heartachingly sweet compared to his usual barrage. I don't know if I'm allowed to move yet or not, so I remain still, my fingers sinking into the carpet as he continues to kiss me with a tenderness that thrums the puppet strings commanding my heart.

Even when showing me kindness, his touch is punishing. I'm out of breath from his kisses, my lips swollen and aching, my jaw tired. He's turning the delicate touch against me, using it as another way to torture me, knowing it's what my sad heart desires the most. Even knowing this is part of whatever wicked game he's playing, I don't want him to stop. My pussy is sore and aching around his still hard dick, and my body hurts, but I'd die happily if I suffocated on his lips. He's pulling away far too soon, his lips glistening as he looks down on me. I can tell from the look in his eye that this night is far from over and it settles the beat of my heart as I stare up at him, waiting for him to say whatever vicious words I know he'll sling at me.

"Thank you, weirdo." It's not what I expected, and it blows like smoke around my heart.

NINE

butterfly kisses

A bunny.

A fucking bunny.

Of all the things my butterfly could have dressed up as for Halloween, she chose one of the most basic bitch outfits. I'm not sure if I'm more annoyed that she's flapping around campus with her fucking tits and ass hanging out, showing off what is *mine* for the entire male population to see, or of her lack of creativity and imagination. Adjusting my top hat, I scan the crowd from my spot on the bench, my eyes landing on my *Thecla betulae* as she chugs from a keg, her bunny ears flopping over her eyes when she stands back up.

It's definitely the lack of brain cells that bothers me most. Unlike her, I actually put thought into my outfit. I have to admit, I've certainly outdone myself this year with my vintage-inspired Jack the Ripper ensemble.

Lucky for my butterfly, the holiday has put me in a rather good mood. It has been my favorite for as long as I can remember. It's the one time of the year that I can be me without all the dramatics; no one is ugly crying or screaming for someone to call the police. The holiday makes people wet with the desire to see wicked things. They laugh and party and drink, all the while watching someone die right in front of their faces, thinking it's a part of the show. The ugly crying doesn't come until well after I've disappeared.

Tonight, I have something exciting planned for my *Thecla betulae*. Something I've been daydreaming about since the idea popped into my head last Halloween. I catch myself smiling whenever I think about it, my heart thumping behind my ribs with anticipation. I have a feeling this will be my favorite collection to date and not because of my butterfly. My eyes find her once more, watching as she grabs the fluffy bunny tail on her naked ass to make sure it's still there. *Where the fuck else would it be?* I've really let my standards slip for this one, I'll admit. She was more of a convenience pick, not like all of my perfect beauties I already have pinned in my shadow box. I'm not sure if spending time with a certain weirdo has something to do with that, or if I was more focused on my actual plan to really care who my prize would be.

It hardly matters though; my butterfly will look just as stunning as the rest.

Just as perfect.

Pulling out my phone, I look at the time. Pretty soon, my butterfly and her group of friends should be heading to the haunted house on the edge of campus. I stand, adjusting my vest before walking in the opposite direction of my *Thecla betulae* and her obnoxious costume. I need to get to the house before she does if I want this plan to work. If she doesn't show up like planned, I'll just have to find a substitution. I've waited way too fucking long for this to just *not* do it. That would seriously piss me off though, so my butterfly's fluffy ass just better be there.

It's about a fifteen-minute walk to the haunted house and I should get there a few minutes before they actually open up for people. If my butterfly leaves when she's supposed to, that'll give me eight to ten minutes to prepare for her. Well, probably longer if she fucks off in the line, which really is likely. Slipping around the back of the building, I bypass the gathering people by the front and open the rear employee entrance. I'm not an employee, but I doubt anyone will stop me. I've found that more often than not, if you act like you belong somewhere, people just believe you. People are so funny in that regard. Everyone is always so trusting.

Grabbing an extra mask, I remove my hat and slip it on before making my way through the dark house. Thanks to visiting the place a few days ago, I already know where I need to go and how it's going to happen. Everything is already in place for me. I also showed up for rehearsals last night to know where all the other people will be hiding for their own scares. Right here, on the second level that overlooks the entrance is where my beautiful but stupid butterfly will make her grand entrance into my collection. My quick, excited breaths are loud inside my mask, and I feel myself smiling again.

I duck back, standing between some large curtains and neon cobwebs as the regular lights shut off, strobes and red bulbs taking their place. Music blares through the strategically placed speakers throughout the house, ghastly howls and screams that add to the ambiance. People have to walk through several rooms of horror down below before they get to the upper level to explore the rooms. Opening an old servants' hallway, I quickly move through the halls to the door at the bottom of the staircase. Besides a few zombie clowns that jump out near the bottom of the stairs, there is nothing but decorations from the stairs to the room on the far left of the upper walkway. I imagine it was a precautionary thing, so that people wouldn't fall down the stairs or over the banister.

The hardest part of this whole thing will be grabbing my butterfly when her group gets scared by the clowns and pulling her back with me without anyone noticing. Theoretically, it shouldn't be that difficult. You can barely see anything, and her screams will get swallowed up with all the others. If by chance I am caught grabbing her, I'll just play it off as part of the entertainment. Opening the door near the end of the staircase, I hide with the other decorations. My mask is getting hot with my adrenaline, my hands starting their tremble of excitement. I almost feel... giddy?

I stand and sweat in place for fucking longer than I anticipated waiting for my butterfly, my doubts that she might not even be coming starting to take over and ruin my mood just as she pops through the doorway. I can barely hear myself think through the pounding of my heart in my ears as I watch her scream over some fake spiders on the floor. I know she'll have to go through the other rooms before I can make my move, but just knowing she's here gets my blood pumping. In approximately twelve minutes, I'll be that much closer to getting my *Thecla betulae*.

Time ticks on so slowly when you're waiting with anticipation and after what feels like an eternity in the dark, my butterfly flutters over toward the staircase. I've timed the zombie clowns with the other groups to know when I can snatch her, and I know that there are three clowns that come out in various positions. I will need to grab her just after the first, so that the group will be too scared and distracted by the second to see me hauling her off. Lucky for me, she's still near the back of her group with an equally naked-looking cat woman, their hands linked as they walk toward me.

I almost feel sick with my excitement, my stomach nauseous as I wait for that first clown. She passes me by a foot and my breath heats up my face as I resist the urge to grab her now. Like clockwork, the first clown jumps out and I make my move. Springing forward, I grab my butterfly around her waist and yank her backward as her startled scream turns into one of true terror, breaking her hold on her friend. Her friend starts to look our way since her hand was tugged but is immediately distracted by the second clown just like I hoped for. Fighting the wiggling woman in my arms, I slam the servant door closed. She's still screaming, her bunny headband falling to the ground as I drag her upstairs. Swinging her sideways, I smack her head on the wall to disorientate her a bit, getting her to stop fighting me as much.

Reaching the second floor, I slap a hand over her mouth as I wait at the doorway, listening for any new groups coming this way. Her group should have passed by now. Hearing the fake chainsaw sound from the kitchen, I know I have about three minutes before that group gets to the clowns below. That means I need to work quickly. Shoving my butterfly forward, I let her hit the floorboards, her arms giving out from under her when I step on her back. I grab the rope I'd laid out yesterday and yank my butterfly's head up enough to secure the noose around her neck. Pulling her up, I fight off her wild swings, letting her hit me a few times as I move her exactly where I want her to be; her back facing the banister as I stick my paper butterfly down the front of her outfit. It won't be displayed nearly as pretty as the others, but it will be tucked away for them to find later. With one final look at my beautiful *Thecla betulae*, I place both palms on her chest and shove. Even in the dark, I see the terror written along her features, her arms wildly swinging to catch herself. To her credit, she almost does, but I push her heeled foot with my own to tip her backward.

And just like that, my butterfly flies.

And it's so unbelievably beautiful.

Screams sound out as the front entrance is opened at just the perfect time to watch her decent, her feet swinging just above their heads in the most theatrical display I've ever managed to create. I hadn't planned on a new group coming in, but fuck, it is *everything*. I can't help but laugh, my hands clapping at my own show. Hearing footsteps coming up the stairs, I sneak back into the hall and shut the door. Opening a door that takes me near the exit, I get rid of my mask and grab my top hat once more. Stepping into the cool fall air, I adjust my vest before leisurely walking away from the haunted house. Everyone here will just assume she's part of the show, a bit that was thrown in at the last minute. It won't be until tomorrow morning when they come to clean the place out that they will realize she's not fake. It will cause mass hysteria among the workers and all the participants who saw her dangling above their heads all night. She will be brought up every Halloween, never forgotten.

My butterfly will be forever memorialized, all because of *me*.

TEN

hadley

"Rivercrest Landing residents are still in shock after Truman employees found the *beloved friend and cheer captain, Jessica Truvinskey, hanging inside of the Truman haunted house last Thursday. Captain Lewis said that they believe her body was being used as a prop for the night's activities and that a large number of people, if not everyone who entered the haunted house, would have seen her. After further inspection of her body, police were able to connect Jessica's murder to eight others in the community after finding what locals have named the calling card for Rivercrest's serial* killer, a butterfly kiss, stuffed inside of her clothing. The Rivercrest police department is urging anyone who may have seen or heard anything in regard to Jessica's death or any of the other's deaths, to call the police hotline listed on the bottom of the screen."

"Thank you, Kathy. Our condolences go toward the family and friends of Jessica and everyone who was forced to be a part of that gruesome event. Understanding how traumatic this could be for some of our Rivercrest Landing residents, the local Seven Day Adventist Church has decided to open its doors and offer its space for some of the area's therapists this Tuesday from eight a.m. to four p.m. Their goal is to provide a safe space for the community to gather and seek comfort, whether it be in praise, comradery or licensed help."

"Susan Baker, administrator for the Rivercrest University psychological wing, has been working in close contact with the Rivercrest police for the last several months, trying to catch the Butterfly serial killer and she had this to say about the recent murder..."

"This guy is smart and he's confident. He most likely isn't going to fit what your ideal thought of a killer would be. All of his victims are educated, pretty, young women which leads us to believe he must either be very charming or very good looking. It's believed at this time that he chooses his victims on a whim as none of the victims' family members have any kind of connective information to make us think he is an active part of their lives. He probably works at the university or somewhere nearby as all of his victims are students or alumni who lived near campus. The best thing you can do to protect yourself is to stay in groups consisting of more than three people, don't go anywhere before or after store and work operating hours, and make sure you lock your doors. Don't assume you're safe because you don't fit his predicted victim catalog. We don't know enough to say for sure he won't deviate. If possible, carry a can of pepper spray on you at all times. The police department is working *around the clock to find this guy, but until then, you need to keep yourself safe."*

I roll over in my bed to face the door, the sound of the television had woken me from the living room as the news anchors continue to speak to each other. Probably not the most relaxing thing to wake up to, but it's a habit I got from my nana. She always had the television set to turn on the second the news started. Mine of course is set for the evening news and not the one that airs at the ass crack of dawn. The Butterfly Killer is all that the news ever talks about these days. As awful as everyone in this town says they think these murders are, they sure bring it up as often as they can. The first murder sent shock waves through the city. The second one had everyone scared to leave their homes. The third caught the attention of the nation, the whisper of Butterfly Kisses flying across the headlines of every major newspaper. The small town of Rivercrest Landing had a serial killer.

It was exciting for people as much as terrifying. Memes started popping up on social media, some of the more promiscuous women advertising themselves as the next victim on social apps. Butterfly Kisses became something people teased each other about even as women continued to be murdered. It's been months since the first kill and the police still have no viable leads. I heard a rumor that the FBI was being brought in, or maybe already had been brought in to help with the investigation, but they clearly haven't found anything.

Sitting up in bed, I toss my covers to the side. Rhys didn't come to the graveyard to sit with me today. He doesn't always, so him not being there wasn't totally weird, but it's the third time this week. He makes regular house calls though, stopping by in the middle of the night to rid his demons on my skin. Some days he's gentler with me, less harsh. And others, he's brutal and relentless, marking my skin with everything in his arsenal. I don't know what causes his shift in mood, what he does all day long that brings him to me the way it does, but I don't care enough to question it. I crave his attention, his desire, and I'll take it in any form he's willing to give it.

I walk over to my dresser, pulling out a pair of black jeans and plain cotton tee shirt and slip them on. Stepping out of my room, my eyes find the television, looking at a commercial for cereal as I grab my hoodie off the back of the sofa. Moving into the kitchenette, I open the fridge, sighing at the three condiments in the door — two slices of processed cheese, and rotten lettuce that looks like I should enter it into the next science fair. Fuck, I need to get groceries. I let the door close, my eyes landing on the oven clock. It's a little after eleven. If I can get to the station in time, I can grab a train to Piggly Wiggly before they close. Decision made, I walk to the door and slip on my sneakers. I'll have to get a new pair soon; these are almost completely worn down. The fabric around my toes is thin and on the verge of getting holes. I don't think they'll make it another winter, but for now, they're fine.

I pat my pocket, making sure I have cash before walking from my place, locking the door behind me.

I barely made it in time to get in and grab a few things before they kicked me out. I could tell the cashier was less than happy to be holding a register open for me even though I made it to him four minutes before they officially closed. I don't blame him though; it was almost midnight, and he was probably ready to be home. Juggling my two grocery bags with one arm and my chest, I reach into my pocket to grab my door key. Unlocking it, I use my foot to push it open, practically throwing my stuff onto the counter before my arms give out, barely saving it all from falling onto the floor.

"You're late."

I jump, knocking one of the bags I just set down. I huff, glaring at Rhys who's lounging on my couch, his bare feet hanging over the edge. Crouching, I start to pick everything up that I knocked down. "How'd you get in here?" Setting everything back onto the counter, I start taking things out of the other bag.

"The door, Hadley. Like most people." He sits up, his feet landing on the floor as he watches me with one eye; long blond shag hiding the other.

"Fucking smartass." I start putting my few groceries away. "The door was locked." I crumble up the bags once they're all put away, tossing them in the trash. He doesn't respond and when I look up, I notice he's watching the television. Kicking my shoes off, I grab them and toss them by the door, moving to drop next to him on the couch. He's sitting directly in the middle of the small couch, not bothering to move when I sit down so I'm squished to the side. "What are you watching?"

"....*ing News. Tracy Mucket, a senior at Rivercrest University, was found murdered in her own home. Detectives say she appears to be another victim of the Butterfly serial killer. RLQ News anchor, Robert Yunder is currently on the scene...*"

"Why are you watching a recording of the news?"

Rhys sits back at my question, his cornflower eyes dropping to my lips. He must be in a fairly decent mood tonight, considering he hasn't mauled me yet or thrown any insults. "It's what was on when I came in and I didn't feel like searching for the remote. Why were you watching it is the real question?"

I had forgotten that I'd left this on the television earlier. "I like watching it. I like knowing what's going on."

"You're a fucking weirdo."

My place is warm, and my hoodie suddenly feels like too much pressed so close to Rhys. I pull my arms from the sleeves and tug it over my head. Shaking it out, I lay it over the side of the couch. "It's not weird to watch the news."

"If you're in your seventies." He's not smiling, but I can hear the humor in his tone.

Running my hands through my hair, my fingers catch on a few tangles. I don't remember the last time I brushed it. "Whatever. Why are you here? Just to watch the news? And why weren't you at the cemetery today?"

"Hadley, shut the fuck up." His fingers grab the front of my shirt, hauling me up onto his lap, my back to his front. His teeth scrape along the shell of my ear, his hot breath puffing along my cheek. "I didn't come here to chat."

My skin immediately responds to him, pebbling with goosebumps. His rough palms dip under my shirt, squeezing and pressing into my skin as they run up my ribcage. I've grown accustomed to his touch; know what kind of fuck he craves based on his first few touches. He's been coming over for weeks now. Never once has he asked me about birth control or protection. I've come to the conclusion he doesn't care. He's not worried about me getting pregnant, because in his mind, it wouldn't be his problem. Of course I can't, but he couldn't know that. I've never told him.

"You're a liar, butterfly." His hot breath dampens the skin of my neck when I turn my face to the side, watching him from the corner of my eye. "You always come here to talk."

His teeth sink into my shoulder, spurring a small hiss to leave my lips. "I think you've become delusional, weirdo."

I shake my head at him, my tongue parting my lips, the scent of him curling around my taste buds making my mouth water. "You may not use your words, but your hands, your mouth, they tell me everything you won't. Every night you visit, I learn more about you. I hear your lies, but I taste your truth."

Rhys's fingers pinch harder into my flesh with every syllable that leaves my lips, but he says nothing, his cornflower eyes glaring down at my profile. I've become bolder with him over the last few weeks. He makes me feel more confident, even if unintentionally. In a way, I find it terrifying, but also exhilarating.

Crossing my arms over my chest, I look forward, grabbing the edge of my shirt to pull over my head and let it fall through my fingers by our feet. Rhys's fingers unclip my bra and I let it fall from my arms. His hands leave my skin and I feel him shift under my butt; his shirt thrown in front of me onto the floor. I lean back into the warmth of his chest, and swallow hard when his palm slides between my breasts to grab my throat. Licking my lips, I let out another bold whisper, swallowing under his palm, "I want to taste your lies, butterfly."

My fingers work the button on my denim as his teeth scrape over my shoulder, his breath making my skin wet. His fingers tighten on my throat when I shift my hips to pull my jeans down, not letting me move away from his chest when I use my feet to pull them off the rest of the way. His wordless response is response enough, his rough fingers digging into my flesh to keep me close. His skin whispers to me what his cruel mouth would never say — he wants me close. He *needs* me close. And my pitiful little heart gobbles up every silent word, etching them into my very soul.

Rhys's hips have started to shift below my ass, his erection grinding into me through his jeans. He doesn't like when I touch him too much, only ever allowing brief swipes of my fingers, so I put my hands on my thighs, biting my lip when his free hand starts to slide down the flat of my stomach. His fingers shove their way under my panties, roughly pressing into my clit with a jerking motion that has the slick of my pussy smacking loudly with each rotation. I widen my legs, bringing them up to straddle his waist from behind, my heels digging into the sides of his legs as he works me with his fingers. I rub against his erection, my slick seeping from my panties to stain the denim between my thighs.

A small sound squeaks through my tight throat and Rhys's teeth sink into my shoulder, drawing another groan. "Louder." I let out the sounds I was suppressing in my chest, each one grumbled and low as it fights to make it past the press of his fingers. The fingers on my clit press harder, my nipples aching tight buds as Rhys continues to place wet hot kisses along my neck and shoulders.

"Louder." My hips rock harder in his lap, the rough denim ripping at my panties with each thrust, scratching my pussy lips with delicious friction. I try to listen to his growled command, but it's difficult with my airway already narrowed under his palm. I try to force the sounds past my lips, my gut warming, spine tingling with my impending orgasm.

"I said louder, Hadley." His voice is dark and gravelly, his swiveling hips meeting my own desperate ones thrust for thrust as we dry hump on the couch. The grip on my throat tightens painfully, almost stopping the scream I manage to work out. It's raspy and deep, my throat burning from the pressure it's under. The slick between my legs is speaking for me, dripping to cover the entire front of his jeans. My vision starts to dot with black, my lungs stinging painfully in my chest as I buck on Rhys's lap.

I orgasm with his tongue on my neck, lapping at a bite as I struggle to stay conscious. His hand drops from my throat just before I think it's too much and I gasp as he takes my hips in his hands, sliding me along his lap to finish dry fucking me. He grinds me down, thrusting so hard the end of his erection juts inside of my pussy lips, denim and all, groaning against my back with his release. It sprays the inside of his jeans, creating another dark wet spot through the fabric. I bring my palm down between my legs, grinding my palm against the spot in a way that has his hips shuddering with too much pleasure below me.

A palm raises to grip my cheeks, turning my head so that his hot tongue can push past my lips to violate the inside of my mouth. Despite the aggressiveness of it, the kiss is surprisingly soft, his breath filling my lungs as I suck up as much of him as I can get. "That's enough." He abruptly shoves me off, my face landing in the cushions as he stands. He looks down at his pants, reaching in to adjust his dick. His eyes find mine as I sit up.

"What're you going to do about your pants?" My voice is hoarse and my throat burns, my chest still heaving to catch my breath.

He shrugs, picking up his shirt off the ground and sliding it over his head. I stare at every beautiful inch of his skin until it disappears below the fabric. "Nothing."

"You're just going to walk around like that?" I gesture toward his pants, and he runs his hands through his hair, pushing the strands, damp with sweat, away from his eyes.

"Yes. I hope they stare too." He walks toward the door, bending to slip into his sneakers. His are just as worn as mine. "So I can tell them I just got done fucking their mom." I suck my lips between my teeth to hide my smile. He grabs his jacket, throwing it on before opening the door. His eyes meet mine as he steps outside. "Later, weirdo."

ELEVEN
butterfly kisses

My *Pyronia tithonus* is striking tonight. Truly stunning with her cream scarf wrapped around her slender neck, the orange copper length of her hair tucked into her coat as the pearlescent gray of her eyes reflects the city line. We're on the top of her building, utilizing the rooftop sitting area for our date tonight. Everything so far has gone smoothly with my butterfly, easy even. Maybe even a little… bland? Possibly boring? I'm not sure if that has to do with my butterfly herself or if it's me.

I'm a collector by nature. There's an unspoken rule that as a collector, you never stop trying to find the best and the newest to add to your existing pretties; and you most certainly don't stop collecting. I have no plans to stop. I think I just need some kind of excitement. Extra spice maybe? My eyes find the copper glow of my butterfly's hair. The beautiful locks are what drew me into her first. It was down and wild around her face, spiraling curls blowing in the breeze. She instantly reminded me of the Gatekeeper butterfly, small and coppery brown. I feel bad for my *Pyronia tithonus.* She's going to think she's the problem here, when really, I've just found myself in quite the funk.

She's currently playing her guitar, quietly humming along with it as she plays me her newest song. She doesn't actually sing. All of her work is instrumental, and I have to say, she's very talented. She wouldn't be mine if she wasn't though, would she? She's a far cry from my latest addition who had the brains of a walnut. Although her show was spectacular, hands down my favorite, I knew I needed a real A+, top-of-the-class kind of butterfly to brighten the box a bit after that one. That's exactly what I found too.

As I sit here, listening to her play, I realize my hands are cold despite the fairly thick leather gloves I'm wearing. My butterfly isn't even wearing any, her fingers plucking away at the strings of her guitar like she doesn't feel the cold. But I know she must, because her cheeks are flushed a pretty shade of baby pink that makes the few freckles on her nose stand out. I truly hate cold weather, even more so when it's windy. Yet here we are, on the top of this building where it is both cold and windy. I really didn't think this date through.

"How'd you like it?"

I almost jump at her voice, blinking to clear my head. I truly am bored if I'm getting lost inside my head like that. "I loved it." I smile at the pleased expression on her face, watching as she sets the guitar off to the side. "You're very talented, butterfly."

She shrugs, sticking her hands between her thighs. So her fingers were cold then. "I'm okay. I need to practice some more to be where I'd like to be."

She's either extremely driven or her parents pushed their own issues on to her to make her think she could always be better. Do better. Some people really shouldn't have kids. What's wrong with not being the best all the time? Literally nothing. In fact, I'd like to think that all of us losers down here are the backbone of the talented. Without us, you'd never know what the true scale of talent was. We're here to be grand examples of what the bottom tier looks like to compare.

"... Professor Angus said that he might be able to get me a spot in his upper musical arts class next semester."

Scrubbing my hand over my brow, I nod at her. I'm not sure how long she's been talking because I got lost in my thoughts once again. What was she talking about? Next semester? Maybe I should tell her she doesn't have to worry about next semester because I plan to rip her wings off. That would definitely make things more interesting, or at least for me. "That would be great."

On a whim, I stand and stretch my hand out toward her. "Have you seen the giant turkey they've set up in the park? I think you can see it from here."

She shakes her head, some of her hair pulling from where it's stuffed in her scarf. "No! I didn't know there was one up."

She takes my hand and I link our fingers, walking with her toward the iron guard railing. Pointing one gloved finger toward the park, I gesture in the direction of the brightly lit up turkey in the distance. Unclasping our hands, I pat my back pocket, intent to pull out a cigarette before I remember I didn't bring them. Well, fuck. My butterfly is talking again, but I'm not listening. What's that show with the trombone sound when all the adults talk? Charlie Brown? That's all I hear coming from her mouth. Wah wah wah.

I'm nodding one moment and then grabbing her arm and pushing her between her shoulder blades the next. It takes me a second to realize I just shoved her over the railing, looking over the edge at her head splattered over the sidewalk. Well, fuck, again. I hadn't planned that. I actually hadn't planned on adding her to my collection for a few weeks yet. I move my face back as a few people run up to her, a woman already screaming something I can barely hear from the eight-story building. Well, butterfly, you may have bored me to death, or yourself to death, but I have to say, you're fucking exquisite.

And she is, with her arms bent and broken in a V shape, like wings, the copper of her hair haloed by a spray of dark red. She's prettier than I could have imagined.

She also doesn't have a butterfly.

Fuck.

Looking around the rooftop, I don't see anything I can even attempt to make one with either. Scrubbing my head with annoyance, I ponder my options. I could leave her without a butterfly, but then no one would know she was mine. Or I could go back down to her apartment and get some paper, hope the cops don't show up before I'm done, and drop it on her. That could work. My mind made up, my feet are already moving toward the rooftop staircase. If I'm quick, I can be in and out of her place within three minutes. She only lives a few floors down and I already know she left her door unlocked for us to get in later, so it shouldn't be difficult.

Opening the doorway to her landing, I accidentally run straight into an older woman carrying what looks like groceries. Grabbing her arms to steady her, I politely shift her out of my way. "I'm sorry. I didn't see you there."

Her freckled hand waves at me, the blue knitted ball on the top of her hat swaying with her shaking head. "Oh, you're fine, honey. Did you just come from the rooftop? It's far too cold to be spending too much time out there."

I nod at her, shifting around her toward my butterfly's apartment a few doors down on the left. "I think I'll be fine. Thanks for the concern."

Quickly walking toward my butterfly's place, I open the door and slip inside. I'm not wildly familiar with her place, but I know she has to have some kind of paper somewhere. Going toward the metal-framed desk in her small living area, I dig around until I find some printer paper. It's thin and extremely boring, but much to my annoyance, it'll have to do. As I'm about to leave, I notice a spread of music sheets.

How perfectly poetic that would be — a butterfly made from her own music. Stuffing the plain butterfly into my pocket, I reach for one of the music sheets and fold that into a small little butterfly instead. The symbolism of it almost makes this drab night exciting. Stepping out of her apartment, I head toward the elevator. I know I need to hurry. I'm sure the police have already been called to the scene and if they aren't there yet, they will be soon. I hate to admit that the thought of being so near to them does seem somewhat exciting, at least compared to how things have been going lately. A close run-in might be just what I need to spice things up.

Pressing the button for the main lobby, I watch the doors close in front of me. Fuck. I should have thought to throw her guitar over after her. That would have made the whole music theme really hit. See, this is why I plan this shit and don't just do things all willy-nilly. This could have been a thousand times better and here I am, throwing my butterfly from her own rooftop because I've suddenly sprung up a case of boredom. The elevator doors open, and I walk through the lobby and out the doors, listening for sirens. I don't hear any, but I can already see the red-and-blue lights flashing from the adjacent street.

Well, fuck again. Pulling my jacket up higher around my face, I tuck my gloved hands into my pockets and walk toward the lights. It's going to be more difficult to get to my butterfly now. Each step has my heart pounding a little harder against my rib cage, that familiar anticipation making my skin prickle. Rounding the corner, I scan the scene. There are two police cars parked on the edge of the street, one officer directing traffic while three others are working to mark the area off from other pedestrians. Well, fuck again, and again. There's also an ambulance, but it looks like the medics are just standing around talking to each other. It's not like they could do much, though. My butterfly's face has been permanently etched into the concrete.

Testing my luck, I continue to walk down the sidewalk. I'm not the only person here; there are others gathering around, whispering behind their hands. Some are even trying to take pictures or videos. My *Pyronia tithonus* has caused quite the commotion, I see. But they won't even know she's mine if I don't get this fucking paper butterfly near her. Squeezing past two women who are crying in shock, I sneak as close as I can to the tape surrounding my butterfly. Even if I tried to throw it from here, I don't think it would make it. Not to mention, everyone would see me throwing it. Grinding my teeth at my own stupidity for being so unorganized, I watch the officers as they talk to one another.

I could put the butterfly on one of them.

It would be risky, but they'd find it later and know. Know she was one of mine.

Know that I was there, watching them.

Know that I touched one of them.

My heart is beating a mile a minute now, my fingers sweating in my gloves. This is exciting again. Now I need to figure out how to get one of them close enough to me to be able to slip it into their jacket pocket. Turning to the women next to me, I try to get their attention. "Do you know what happened?"

Sniffling, she looks over at me, shaking her head. "Some girl just jumped. I don't think we know her, but Mia said she has red hair like our friend, Sarah, who also lives in the building."

Well, it definitely isn't Sarah, but I'm not going to reassure them of that. "I know Sarah. Wasn't she having relationship issues?" I have no idea if she was or not, but considering most college women are, I figured it was a good shot at getting these two worked up.

One of them gasps, both of their eyes going wide. Bingo. "Oh my God! You don't think she would have jumped, do you? I thought she and Steven made up?!"

I just shrug, shaking my head as I look back out at my butterfly, now covered with a silver blanket to keep her from sight. "I don't know. She was pretty broken up over something when I talked to her."

They both start crying again, one of them leaning from her friend's grip to yell toward the police. "Sarah! I need to see if that's Sarah!" She pulls from her friend, her hand reaching out to grab the yellow tape in front of us. "Please, I need to see if it's her!"

One of the officers breaks from their huddle, jogging our way to stop the woman from dipping under the tape. "Ma'am, we know you're concerned, but we need you to stay on the other side of the tape."

"No, I need to see if that's my friend. Her name is Sarah. I need to see if that's her." She tries to fight from his grip, and I pull my hands from my pockets, stepping forward to grab her arm in an act of trying to keep her back. Before pulling her away, I slip my little butterfly into the officer's unzipped jacket pocket. I keep my face sideways as I talk to her, my profile to the officer as I keep her back. "You'll find out, but you can't go in there. If it is her, you wouldn't want to see her like that anyway."

She lets me pull her back and her friend grabs her arm once more, cooing to her things I can't hear, but also don't care to. I've accomplished what I needed. Turning from them, I walk back down the street. My heart is still pumping from the adrenaline of doing something so risky, but I can't deny how exciting that was. Too exciting. If I'm not careful, I'll walk myself right into getting caught just for a fucking thrill.

TWELVE

hadley

We're at the cemetery again, Rhys and me. It seems we're always here, him more so now than he was before. He's around a lot, actually. I'm scared to admit what that means to my lonely desperate heart. It's dangerous for him to give someone like me so much attention, simply because I don't know if I could ever survive again without it. I don't know how Rhys feels about me, but I know that I need him. In many ways, needing something, in the desperate, chaotic way that I need, is even more powerfu

I need the intimacy he offers, no matter how cruel and twisted. I need the comfort he provides by not leaving me alone. I need to feel wanted in the same way he makes me feel it. He gives me a sense of purpose again. A sense of self-worth. I realize how shallow that sounds to most; the idea that I need this wicked strange man to feel worthy, the same man who fucks for his own pleasure, smiles at my pain, and slings insults more times than compliments. I simply don't care how it looks to others because at least one person, no matter how vile, mean, or cruel, finds me worthy. *Me.* And I know he feels the same even if his twisted lips won't admit it.

Standing from my usual spot at Nana's grave, I look down at Rhys. Something about him feels off from the last time I saw him. I couldn't say why because he hasn't necessarily acted any different than usual, it just seems to be something I know. I can almost feel it. My mood stone has been swirling between brown and periwinkle like it can't make up its mind. Grabbing my backpack, I put a strap over my shoulder. "You hungry?"

Rhys's teeth slide along his lower lip at my question, his eyes working their way from my worn sneakers, slowly up to my face. "I might be."

I don't need to look at my mood stone to know it's turned dark pink at his tone. I don't think he's referring to the same type of hunger as I am. "For food, Rhys. Do you want to get something to eat?"

A loud breath blows from his lips, his baby blues rolling as he stands. I watch as he steps up to my chest, his thumb swiping over my lower lip, roughly grating it against my teeth before his hand drops. "I'll go with you, if that's what you're asking."

"It is." I want him to kiss me, even if it's just with his teeth. But I don't want to ask, so I turn away from him instead, squishing a dandelion into the grass as I start to walk away.

I am jerked backward by my backpack, my feet stumbling over themselves as I try to regain my footing. Bright blond hair and cornflower eyes drop into view as my face is yanked to face the sky by my short ponytail. "If you want a kiss, Hadley, all you have to do is ask."

His lips land on mine in the next breath, his top teeth lightly scraping against my lower lip as he kisses me. The angle hurts my neck and back, but I don't fight it, my left hand rising to touch him. He pushes me away before my fingers make contact, the tips just brushing along a few wild strands. I stumble forward and he chuckles as he passes me. I don't know how he knew I wanted a kiss. I didn't think I'd been that obnoxiously obvious, but I have zero complaints.

I follow him, intermittently watching his back as we walk. He glances over his shoulder at me. "Where are we going?"

I shrug even though he's already facing forward and can't see it. "The diner on Fifth Avenue?"

"Are you asking me or saying that's where you want to go?" He pulls a cigarette from his pocket, and I look over as we pass a couple placing flowers on a tombstone.

Smoke blows behind his head to tease my nostrils. "That's where we're going."

Following the orders of the *Seat Yourself* sign, we find a spot in the back of the diner at the very end of the submarine-shaped space. Everything is very stereotypically decorated — yellow-and-red seats and tables, striped uniforms, and an open kitchen. It's old-fashioned and maybe a little disgusting if you look too closely at things, but the atmosphere is homey. Grabbing a "daily specials" menu from between the ketchup and mustard bottles, I peek at Rhys over the laminated edge.

I'm guessing since it's laminated, the daily specials are the same every day.

"Are you going to look at the menu or keep being a weirdo?" His eyes find mine as he settles back in his seat, and I purse my lips. He wasn't even looking at me.

A waitress walks by, her arms full with two trays of food and a wide smile cast our way. "One minute, honey, and I'll be right with you."

I offer her a small smile, turning my attention back to the menu. Dinner decided, I slip it back between its spot by the condiments. "Are you not getting anything?"

Rhys shakes his head, his fingers tapping on the back of the booth. "I'm going to smoke." He slips from the booth as I watch him, my heart picking up just the slightest bit at the thought that he might be ditching me. It shouldn't matter, but it does. His hand reaches out to chuck under my chin, the straight line of his teeth peeking from between his lips. "I'll be right back."

The touch was hardly sweet, but my chin chases after his fingers as he pulls them away. "Okay." Twisting in my seat, I watch him walk out the door. I can just barely see him standing on the other side of it.

Turning back around, my hands twist in my lap as I wait for the waitress to come back. Looking out the window to my right, my reflection stares back at me. Raising a hand, I smooth a few flyaways that have managed to escape my ponytail and pull the sleeves of my hoodie over my palms when I look away. The waitress from before pops in front of the table with a glass of water that is set in front of me, and I return the smile she gives me.

"What can I get you, honey?" Her pen is ready at her notepad, her pretty brown eyes shifting to look at another booth when someone raises their hand.

"Uh, can I get the club sandwich?"

"Sure, what kind of side do you want? Chips or fries?" Her eyes bounce between my face and the notepad.

"Fries, please."

"Got it. Anything else? Something besides water?"

My eyes shift from her to look out the front door where I last saw Rhys. "Water is fine, but can you bring another glass?"

She nods, tucking her pen and notepad into the apron wrapped around her waist. "Of course. Is someone meeting you? I can hold on to your order until they get here."

Frowning, I shake my head at her. "No, he's already here. He's just outside."

"Oh! I didn't see anyone here with you, but I'm running on two hours of sleep so that could explain it. Sorry, honey. I'll get your food out for you and get that water brought over."

She spins away from me with another smile, moving toward another booth. She's clearly sleep deprived but seems nice. Another ten minutes or so go by, and she sets a glass of water and my food onto the table with a quick "Let me know if you need anything else," just before Rhys comes back inside. I didn't see him come back in, but he flops into the booth across from me, smelling like tobacco and smoke.

"You were outside a while." I take a bite of my fry, watching him watch me. We've never done anything like this before, something as mundane as eat in public. Seems like neither one of us knows how to act.

His arms stretch onto the back of his seat as he leans back, a smirk on his lips. "Tell me more about your nana."

I swallow down my fry, picking my sandwich up with a slight shake in my fingers and a yellow glow in my ring. "Why are you so interested in her?"

He shrugs, his eyes wandering over the other people in their booths. "I sit on her grave with you almost every day. Seems like I should get to know the lady."

Taking a bite, I consider his answer. I guess it makes sense. "I moved in with my nana after the fire. I had only met her a few times before that, so it was weird at first, but my nana was a very persistent lady. She burrowed and wormed her way into my trust. She was kind, probably one of the kindest people I've ever met. She was always trying to help people, always lending a hand whenever she could. I don't know how she did it, but she somehow made everyone feel important. She had a way about her that just called to people." I eat a fry, my gut feeling tight and nauseous over the conversation. "She made me feel wanted and loved and accepted from the moment I stepped into her life, even if it took me a bit to trust what I was feeling."

Rhys's eyes follow my hand as I grab my glass of water, flicking from my fingers to my face.

"Why didn't you know her before that? Before the fire, I mean."

Setting the glass down, I trail my finger through the wet ring of condensation that's accumulated on the tabletop. "From what I could get out of Nana, she and my father weren't close."

"Why?" My chest pinches at his question, my eyes slightly narrowing. He knows this isn't a subject I like to talk about and he's deliberately pushing my boundaries.

"I don't know."

His arms drop from the back of the seat, his elbows resting on the tabletop. "I think you do."

I push my plate off to the side, no longer hungry because of the conversation. "How could you possibly know what I know? How could you know anything?" I realize my voice has raised to an inappropriate level with my anxious anger, and a few heads turn my way. I force back a low breath to calm myself. I'm letting him work me up over nothing.

"You're telling me you really have absolutely no idea?" He's goading me, a smirk twisting his face into something ugly and cruel.

"No. I don't."

He must hear the finality in my voice because he leans back again, lips settling into a line. "What started the fire then? If you're not going to give me the juicy details of your family drama, then you got to give me something."

I huff, my eyes looking anywhere but at him as that knot in my stomach increases. "I don't have to give you anything, actually."

He flicks the side of my head, forcing my gaze to his face. "Come on, Hadley, spill your dirty secrets for me." He leans over the table, his chest pressed into the edge so he can whisper into my face. "Who started the fire, weirdo?"

I jerk out of the booth the second the words pass his lips, and he cackles at my reaction, standing as I angrily grab my backpack and toss cash onto the table. Turning without looking at him, I stomp past all the other booths toward the exit. My waitress says something to my back, but I don't hear it, pushing outside into the cold. I know Rhys is following me. I can feel him right on my heels, but I don't look. At least not until he grabs my wrist at the back of the parking lot and forces me to.

"Come on, you know I'm joking."

I stare at the zipper on his jacket, refusing to look into his face. I'm angry without a doubt, but also confused by my reaction. I don't know why I don't want to answer his questions, but for some reason I can't. I don't think I could get the words past my lips even if I wanted to. The thought alone makes me nauseous. "Well, it wasn't funny. Not to me."

His fingers pinch into my skin as he lifts my jaw, bringing my eyes off his chest and to his face. "I didn't peg you for a crybaby." I slap his hand away, trying to get away from him but he doesn't let me. My hoodie is fisted at my chest, and I'm tugged up onto my toes, his angry dark eyes meeting mine. "Get your shit together, Hadley. If you lose it, we both do."

He lets go of me, letting me stumble forward as he steps out of my space and out of reach. He turns away from me without another word, disappearing as I stand there in the dark parking lot, wondering what the fuck just happened.

THIRTEEN

butterfly kisses

"**O**rder twenty-seven!" a waitress yells from the take-out counter, order receipt in hand as she scans the room.

Stepping up to the counter, I set my number card by the register. "That's me."

She smiles, peeking into the bag. "Two chicken Alfredo kits with extra sauce and a garlic loaf?"

With a nod, I reach for the bag. "Sounds right."

"Great." Making sure I've got it, she lets go of the bag and steps back as I start to walk away. "Have a good night!"

I raise my fingers in thanks, weaving through the other people waiting for their food. The cold hits my face as my feet meet the sidewalk and I shiver against it. Standing inside made me forget how cold it was out here. We haven't had any snow yet, but I'm sure it's coming. You can almost feel it in the air. I loathe it. Any day we don't have the wretched white fluff is a day I'm grateful for. Thankfully, I don't have to walk far because I'm renting a loft not far from the restaurant.

Opening the front door, I hurry inside, toeing my sneakers off before walking into the kitchen to set my take-out bag on the counter. My butterfly should be here shortly, and I'm supposed to be making her dinner, which is why I ordered takeout. Taking the chicken Alfredo kits out of my take-out bag, I pull out two bowls and start dumping it in. All the noodles go into one and the chicken sauce goes in the other, along with the extra containers of sauce. Setting the oven to one-hundred-and-fifty degrees, I pull the garlic bread out and unwrap it from the aluminum wrapping before sticking it in to keep it warm. Scooping up the containers and foil, I put it back inside the white take-out bag, tie it shut, and shove it to the bottom of the trash can under the sink. Looking at the food on the counter, I mentally pat myself on the back. It may not be the most impressive display, but it's bound to impress my butterfly. I even ordered from the best Italian place in the city.

There's a light knock on the door and I hurry to the front door, taking a second to look through the peephole to verify it's my *Aglais io*. I smile as I open the door and she lifts her hand with a small, somewhat awkward finger wave. "Hey."

Opening the door, I smile at her, stepping back to let her in. "Hey." I shut the door after her, my hand reaching for the coat she's removed while watching her bend over to slip out of her tall boots. "You hungry? Food is ready but we can wait if you're not."

"I'm actually starving. I missed lunch by accident." Standing straight, she uses two fingers to push her glasses back up her nose. The amber frame highlights the bright blue of her eyes and I take a moment to admire her as she removes her scarf. The pairing is what I like most about her, so reminiscent to the European Peacock butterfly with its amber wings and blue spots. I hang her coat and scarf on the hook as she speaks, "What're we having? It smells good."

She's right, it does smell good, but that's mostly the garlic bread heating in the oven. "Chicken Alfredo and garlic bread."

She smiles. "It sounds good too." There's a dining table set up just off the kitchen, visible from the living room and I walk her there.

Walking back to the living room, I pick up the television remote and turn it on for noise, not bothering to check the channel. "Do you want me to dish you up?"

She rests her chin on her hand, her eyes on the television when she answers, "Sure."

Tossing the remote onto the couch, I walk to the kitchen. Grabbing two plates from the cupboard, I put noodles on the plates, then take the bread out and slice it, adding a piece to each plate. Peeking around the arched doorway into the dining room, I make sure my butterfly is still watching television before grabbing a bottle of strychnine pills from my pocket. Tonight, I'm trying something I've never done before in an attempt to reclaim some of that excitement I seem to be craving lately.

It's slightly nerve-racking that I don't know for certain if this will work or not, but it adds to my thrill. Of course I don't want things to go wrong, but it's exciting to think it might and I'll have to use Plan B to take care of things. Unscrewing the cap on the bottle, I dump half the bottle onto the counter. Using the flat side of my knife, I crush them up until they're the texture of dust, then sprinkle it onto the top of my *Aglais io's* plate of noodles. Eyeing the powder, I'm not sure how much she actually needs for it to work. On a whim, I dump the other half out and crush it then add it with the rest.

Scooping out the sauce, I pour a generous serving on her plate to hide the powder, mixing it in with her noodles to make sure everything gets coated. Putting the cap back on the empty bottle, I stick it back in my pocket. Using a clean spoon, just to be safe, I pour sauce over my noodles. Grabbing two forks, I set them on our plates before picking them up, careful to keep my butterfly's in my left hand. How disappointing it would be to kill myself while trying to catch a thrill.

I set the plate in front of her, nodding at her "Thank you" while I put my own plate on the opposite end of the table. Realizing I forgot to get us drinks, I start to stand, but she stops me. "Have you heard about this?" She points to the television, and I look over at it. It's the news channel and they're talking about the Rivercrest Landing serial killer. My heart flutters. It's always so fun to see myself on television. I'm practically a celebrity around here based on how often my name gets brought up. "And people are calling the little butterflies he leaves butterfly kisses." She shudders like the thought creeps her out and I frown. "That's so weird."

And that's so rude.

I stop myself from saying anything, watching as she twirls some pasta around her fork. She takes a bite and I hold my breath with anticipation.

"Did you make this?" she asks while taking another bite. At my nod, she picks up her garlic bread. "It's really good, but not as good as my mom's."

I blink at her, letting go of the breath I was holding since it's obvious she isn't about to keel over. I have to say, I hadn't noticed until now how rude my little butterfly was. "Nothing ever is." I take a bite of my own food, watching her fork like a hawk. "You can never beat a mom's home cooking." As if I would even know, my mother had hardly ever cooked.

She points her fork at me as she chews, nodding in agreement. "I think it might just need some more salt," she says around a mouthful of garlic bread.

My palms are starting to get sweaty as I watch her eat, my eyes narrowing with each bite she takes that doesn't make her keel over. Did I not add enough? Did it get diluted with the food? I should have just shoved it down her snotty little throat. "I'll keep that in mind for next time." I try not to snap it at her, smiling to hide the irritation lining my voice. I didn't make the food so her critiques shouldn't bother me, but it annoys me anyway.

I didn't realize my butterfly was fucking Martha Stewart.

I slurp down some of my noodles, my tongue running over my teeth after I swallow. Just when I start to think this whole thing was a lost cause, my butterfly jerks in her seat. Her hands rise to her face as she starts to smile; a hard, forced-looking smile with pinched cheeks. I don't think it's one she's willingly making. Her body starts to shake, her limbs jerking uncontrollably in the chair. Small gurgling sounds are coming from her stretched mouth as her arm knocks her Alfredo onto the floor. I slap my hand on the table, a laugh bubbling up from my chest as she continues to shudder across from me.

And here I was doubting myself. I should've known better.

Her hands seem to have gotten stuck near her face and throat, her elbows jutting out like

209

beautiful broken wings. Her back is spasming, her body only staying upright because of the arms on her chair and the table's edge. My butterfly is purely divine as she flutters in her seat, the bright blue of her eyes shining like orbs of sapphire. Her glasses have been knocked askew on her head, so I push back in my seat, walking over to her. Grabbing the frames, I adjust them on her shaking body, brushing some of the hair from her face that has fallen from her ponytail. "That's better."

Moving back to my seat, I scoot back up to the table and pick up my fork. Taking a bite, I nod at my butterfly. "You know, the food tastes better now and I can't quite put my finger on why." I smile to myself as she rocks and jerks in her chair. "Earlier, when you said the butterfly kisses are weird, that hurt my feelings, *Aglais io.*" I take a bite out of my bread, swiping it through some sauce. "I put a lot of effort into finding my butterflies. Every one of you is special to me. You're all unique and talented. Beautiful." I pick up my last piece of chicken, swiping it through the remaining sauce. Chewing, I watch my butterfly across the table, still fluttering for me. "I love my butterflies more than anything in this world."

Pushing my plate away, I sit back, crossing my finger as I lean back in my chair. "I pick my paper butterflies to match their real-life counterparts. Each fold in that paper is a layer of my love and adoration. Each crease is my undying loyalty. They're my promise to always love you, always cherish you in my collection. Those paper butterflies are a symbol to everyone else that you are mine." I lick my lips, smiling at my butterfly. I knew it would take a good amount of time for her to leave me, but she's a fighter. "As mine, it's my duty to take care of you and keep you safe from the cruel, dark world we live in. The only way for me to do that, is to keep you in here." I tap my chest, two fingers digging into my skin to tap where my heart sits below my ribs. "My heart, where you've always belonged. Forever immortalized. Forever cherished. Forever loved."

I stand once more, walking over to my butterfly still jerking in her chair. Her legs have almost coiled around the chair's wooden legs, her socked toes curled underneath her feet. My knuckles run along her twitching cheek. I can hear her breaths wheezing from between her clenched teeth. It probably won't be long now before she leaves me. "I'm doing this for you, butterfly." A few tears have leaked down her cheeks, a drop forming at the corner of her eye that I wipe away. I smile down at her, so happy with my butterfly's performance. "Before you go, I think you should know the truth." I pause, brushing another tear away. "I didn't make dinner. I bought it."

Moving away from her, I grab her plate of food, then my empty one, taking both to the kitchen. Setting mine on the counter, I pull out the trash can and dump my butterfly's leftovers into the can. Setting her plate in the sink with mine, I grab all the extra food bowls and the garlic bread and throw it away as well. After removing the bag and setting it off to the side, I put the can back under the sink. I rinse off the dishes with the sponge sitting beside the faucet before inserting them in the dishwasher, making sure to set the water temperature to hot and sanitize. Grabbing a spare rag from the drawer and a bottle of all-purpose cleaner, I spray down the countertops and appliances, making quick work of wiping down all the surfaces I've touched.

Walking into the living area with my rag, I wipe down the door handle both inside and outside, spray the remote, clicking off the television before I clean it off and drop it back onto the couch. Moving toward my now still butterfly, I carefully remove her glasses, using my rag to wipe down the frames before placing them back on her smiling face. I wipe down the table and chairs, and even my butterfly just to be safe.

Moving back to the kitchen, I wipe off the spray bottle, opening the cabinet with my rag before using it to set the bottle inside and close the door. Lastly, I bring my rag to the washer, setting it to hot just like the dishwasher, using my rag to turn the knobs before tossing it in and bumping the lid shut with my elbow.

Taking my orange-and-blue paper butterfly from my pocket, I find my way back to my butterfly. Her fingers are still twitching on and off, but I know she's been dead for quite some time. Placing the paper butterfly on the table in front of her, I admire her a moment longer. Her performance was stunning, like all of them were. Perfectly executed. I'm pleasantly surprised that my first poisoning went so well, yet I didn't quite reach that level of excitement I've been looking for. This wasn't thrilling. My blood didn't pump in my veins. My heart didn't bang so hard against my ribs that it felt like it might burst. My hands didn't tremble with excitement, nor did I completely lose my breath. All those things that used to happen when I first started my collection.

Backing from the room, I spin on my heel toward the kitchen once more to grab the trash bag before heading toward the door. Slipping my sneakers on, I throw on my jacket and gloves. Opening the door, I lock it from the inside before shutting it. Pulling the loft key from my pocket—already wiped clean and secured in an envelope—I drop it into the locked mailbox hanging by the door. Spinning away, I toss my hood over my ears to hide my head from the cold breeze and carry the trash bag over to the neighbor's bin sitting by their driveway. It'll get picked up by morning that way. Tucking my gloved fingers into my pockets, I start on the five-block walk back to where I parked my car.

I don't think I'm disappointed with tonight, but I'm not satisfied either. I tried something new and despite all the signs pointing to it being what I've been lacking, it just fucking wasn't. I can't shake the hollowness in my gut, can't scratch the itch on my back. I'm missing something but I can't figure out what.

I need more.

But more of what?

FOURTEEN

hadley

"**H**adley!"

Pausing on the sidewalk, I look around, thinking someone called my name. When I don't hear it again, I keep walking.

"Hadley! Hey, hold up." Kyler runs up behind me, his hand resting on my shoulder. He smiles, slightly out of breath and I shift so his hand falls. "I haven't seen you in a while."

I nod, stepping out of the middle of the sidewalk and shifting my backpack on my shoulders. "Yea, I've been busy."

He moves with me, crossing his arms over his chest. "Are you working now or something?"

I shake my head. "I mean, no. I just do that arts-and-crafts class at the retirement home still."

"Then why are you busy?"

I frown at him, my lips pursing. "I just am. Did you have something in specific you wanted to say? Because I'm on my way home and don't really feel like catching up."

His arms drop to his sides as he nods. "Right. I was just going to say that Joshua saw you at that diner on Fifth Avenue the other day." I wait for him to elaborate, blinking at him until he does. "He said you seemed pretty angry about something."

I scoff, my hands finding the straps of my backpack. "I was there with Rhys, a... friend of mine. He went outside to smoke for a while then came back inside. As for being angry, you can mind your own business."

I start to walk around him, but he stops me, his hand touching my arm. "No, you're right. I'm sorry."

"Bye, Kyler." I shake off his arm and walk away. He doesn't follow me and I'm grateful for it. Despite how much he tries, we aren't close like that, and I have no plans to be.

I'm just coming up on my house when I spot a familiar face hiding in the dark. "There you are." It's said from the shadows, Rhys's familiar growl reaching out to blow in my ear as he stands from the tree he was leaning against. I don't look at him and I don't stop walking, but he doesn't care. "I thought you'd be home sooner."

"Thought wrong." I can already tell by his tone that he's not in the mood for my games, but I can't help it.

He grabs my backpack, yanking me backward by the handle on top. I'm spun to face him and his lips glide over mine, soft and sweet for all of three seconds. Biting into my lower lip, he tugs it back,

221

letting it scrape through his teeth as he lets it go. "Run."

I blink up at him, confused by his quiet demand. "What?"

He releases me, the white blond of his hair reflecting off the moon at his back. "Run, Hadley."

It only takes me a second to react, my sneakers scraping on the sidewalk as I spin around and take off for my backyard. Stepping off the sidewalk, I cut through the grass, sprinting toward my open yard gate. I can hear Rhys's footfalls behind me, and my heart picking up has nothing to do with my running. I ditch my backpack at the gate, swinging it off my shoulders and tossing it toward the side of my house. Pumping my arms, I sprint across my back lawn, knowing I'm getting closer and closer to getting caught.

I feel his presence before his big hand knuckles the back of my hoodie, catching me off balance. I'm slammed to the ground, Rhys's body following mine as I'm rolled to lie on my back. Rhys's forearms lock on either side of my head, his hair hanging down as he looks at me, legs tangled with mine. Both of us are breathing heavily, our chests almost in tune as he braces above me.

"Your sex kinks are really weird."

His upper lip curls at my remark, his tongue reaching out to lick the seam of my upper lip. "You would know."

I laugh at that, the sound carrying through the trees. My house is the last on the cul-de-sac. You can't even see the other houses from my driveway, and it bumps up right onto the Rivercrest National Forest. We're completely secluded out here. It's cold though. My fingers and face feel tingly with the chill. "You caught me, now what?"

He sits up instead of answering, his hands pulling off my sneakers. I frown at him, watching his fingers find the button on my denim. He starts to tug them down and I try to grab them with no success. "I'm going to freeze out here!"

He shrugs, his piercings glinting in the moonlight. "You should have run into the house." He jerks my jeans over my feet, his eyes on my pussy as his hands slide up my thighs. "Take your hoodie off."

Already shivering, I do as he says, pulling it over my head and discarding it off to the side. My skin is pebbled with goosebumps, the cold air stinging my flesh. His big warm hands slide up my sides, pushing my shirt along with it. I raise my arms, letting him pull it up and over my head. He nods at my bra, and I silently slip it off. I'm shivering before him, my arms crossing over my chest to get warm.

He shakes his head and I drop them, knowing that fighting him gets me nowhere. He spreads my legs wide as he kneels before me, his hands running over my knees and down my thighs. His touch is different tonight, no less rough but somehow more gentle than usual. The way his fingers bump along my scars as he admires them makes my belly heat. The way his eyes soak up every inch of me like he's memorizing every blemish makes my heart thump. Using his thumbs, he spreads my pussy lips, groaning at the soft, wet sound that his fingers make. The noise curls my toes into the grass. His attention moves upward at a leisurely pace as he draws out his movements, his fingers plucking at the already hard peaks of my nipples until my fingers are digging into the grass beside me.

He leans over me, and I suck in his warmth, moaning into his mouth as he takes my lips in his, licking the taste of me from my tongue. His teeth lightly scrape my chin as he pulls away, wet kisses placed on my neck and collarbone that burn in the cold air. "Touch yourself."

I immediately respond to his low whispered command, my hand snaking between our bodies to stroke my cold fingers along my hot wet slit. I circle them around my clit, arching into Rhys's mouth as he sucks in a nipple, flicking his tongue until it's oversensitive and I'm wiggling beneath him. He gives the other breast equal treatment, his warm hands running along my goosebumps, overstimulating with my tight nipples and pumping fingers. He sits back and I watch as he unzips his denim, pushing it down far enough to free the long, hard length of his erection. He runs his hand down the length, his palm squeezing over the head as his eyes fix on my fingers sliding in and out of my slick pussy.

He's taking his time with me tonight, drawing out every movement. If I'm not careful, I might let it go to my head, let myself believe that this cruel man might actually care for me.

The hand wrapped around his dick matches my rhythm, continuing to fuck his hand as he watches me masturbate for him. A small bit of precum squirts out of the tip of his penis onto his fingers and I moan at the sight, my palm working my clit as I lift my hips off the ground for him. The sight of his fingers spreading the cum over his swollen head has my pussy clenching the air in search of his dick. I part my lower lips for his dark gaze, wordlessly inviting him to slip in, spreading them with the fingers of one hand while I thrum my clit with the other. My hips shift to fuck the air as I silently beg him to fill me up, my tits squished between my arms so they jiggle with each small move I make.

I almost cry when he moves forward, his eyes meeting mine as he grabs my hips and slides me to him. I can't keep my hips still as he lines his dick up with my soaking pussy, my hands ripping at the grass on either side of me as I wait for him to fill me up. I barely feel the cold anymore, all my attention and focus on the tip of his dick pushing between my lower lips. He presses a palm on my lower belly, fucking me with just the tip of his dick as I moan my frustrations into the trees.

"That's a good girl." He's biting his lip, a scowl in place as he watches the swollen head of his dick disappear between my wet lips. It's the first real praise he's ever given me, and I almost combust with the rush it gives me, my heart thrumming as he continues to tease me. I want all of him, but I know better than to ask. Even with his newfound kindness, I know he'll refuse just to spite me, even if it's something he also wants.

I'm on the cusp of my orgasm, the back of my spine warming, moving toward my gut as I thrust in the grass below Rhys. He chooses that moment to ram me full with the rest of his length and I instantly orgasm, my pussy clenching around him as he groans above me. I thrust through my release, his palms pressing down on my inner thighs to keep me spread for him as he jerks into me with an almost mindless rhythm. I can vaguely feel that my toes are frozen, but I don't even care anymore, watching Rhys's hair flop over his eye as he groans out his release between my thighs. His tongue runs over his bottom lip as he looks down at me, his hips pumping leisurely a few more times before he pulls out.

All we ever do is fuck and part of me hates that. But another part of me knows that's all I could ever get from Rhys. All *anyone* could ever get from him. And knowing that somehow makes it feel more special than it probably is.

I watch him as he tucks himself away, his eyes raking over my body like he's not finished for the night. He reaches over and grabs my hoodie, tossing it to me. "You should get dressed. Your lips are starting to turn blue." He smirks at that, standing as he watches me cover back up.

I pull my panties back on and my hoodie, but just grab the rest. As I stand, Rhys's eyes follow me and I start walking toward my house. Pushing open the sliding door, I walk in, leaving it open for him. He closes it behind him, leaning against the glass. Shivering, now that I'm not thoroughly distracted, I grab a blanket and sit on the couch. I have to rest my cheek on the cushioned headrest to see Rhys.

"You never talk about yourself."

His eyes narrow marginally, his big body moving off of the door to sit on the couch with me. He pushes my feet off his lap when I try to set them there and I bite back a smile. Rhys is definitely not a cuddly guy. "Why should I? You already know everything about me."

I scoff, watching as he grabs the remote from the coffee table to flick the television on. "That's not true."

He looks at me from the corner of his eye. "You know it is." His tone says the conversation is over, so I scoot lower onto the couch, resting my head on my arm as a pillow. My eyes are just starting to drift closed when I feel the soft swipe of Rhys's thumb on my ankle under the blanket.

"Go to sleep, Hadley." Knowing he'll stop if I say anything, I just smile to myself and go to sleep.

FIFTEEN

butterfly kisses

I dreamt about this. It was one of those dreams that almost feels like a whisper of a memory. Like a sense of Déjà vu. I wasn't going to actually put it into action, but the more I tried to suppress it, the harder it lingered. Like a spot on the carpet, you just can't scrub out. The more and more you scrub, it just gets bigger, spreading further and further until it is worse than it was when you started and simply can't be ignored. I found myself focusing more on the dream and the need to reenact it than the butterfly

I'd be adding to my collection. She is still important, just not quite as important.

Maybe my unfixable case of unfulfillment dreamed it up for me as a solution to the problem I haven't been able to fix. It certainly is bound to attract attention. Or, and most likely, I'm teetering on the edge of desperation to feel that thing I seem to be missing. Like slurping down a slushy a tad too quickly, all I can manage is a rapid and short brain freeze instead of the high I'm looking for. I feel like I've left the house and forgotten something, but I can't remember what it is I've forgotten.

This looming in my gut makes me sick.

Finding the butterfly to fit my ideal vision was easy enough. My butterflies always find me. They know they belong to me and eventually always flutter straight in my direction. I'm the dark desire they want, and they don't know why. Usually, I'm their dirty secret as much as they are mine. Not for the same reasons of course, but it works in my favor nonetheless, so I try not to let it bother me too much.

Although my vision for tonight doesn't require that much planning in regard to preparation, it feels important to get as many details as I can right. That includes my *Vanessa carduii*. My dream didn't have a clear appearance for her, but a blurry idea that she was tall and slender with long brown hair. In a way, generic, but still beautiful like all the butterflies in my collection.

"I think I'm ready to leave." *Vanessa carduii* links her gloved fingers with mine, her breath puffing out in front of her face. We've been in her neighboring park, looking at the ice sculptures for a while now. It's almost midnight, so the park is quiet and peaceful, the sculptures looming in the shadows of the lamps above. "I'm freezing, look." She flashes her teeth in a wide, grimacing chattering smile.

I smile at her, tugging her closer so that I can loop my arm over her shoulder, our joined fingers resting against her arm. "I agree, it's cold. My toes have been frozen in my sneakers for the last thirty minutes."

She snorts, her other hand adjusting the fluffy hat on her head. "I told you to wear something other than your sneakers in the snow."

I hum in acknowledgment, my eyes trailing the string of Christmas lights lining the fence we're walking past. "You did." My breath curls around my face, trailing behind me as we walk. "I should have listened."

"Do you even own a pair of boots?"

I shrug, letting go of her fingers so I can tuck my gloved hands into my pockets. "Probably."

She laughs, the sound traveling around the empty, cold street. "How do you not know?"

I return her smile, flashing icicle lights glinting in her eyes as we go by. "I don't wear them often enough to know for sure."

Her head shakes, her chocolate-brown braid swinging back and forth with the movement. "You're silly."

I give her a look, but don't respond. Reaching in front of her, I open the gate to her yard, letting her go ahead of me. Following behind her, I watch her open her door and step inside, her hand holding it open for me. Walking in, I shut it with my foot, keeping my sneakers on instead of leaving them by the door like usual. My butterfly hurriedly shucks off her coat and boots, her gloves peeled back and stuffed into her jacket pocket where it's hung on the wall. It's not until she turns to look at me, rubbing her hands together to warm up that she notices I haven't taken anything off.

"What're you doing? Aren't you staying?" Her brow pinches with her question, her eyes blinking at me from the end of the foyer.

Unfortunately for my butterfly, there was one thing that stood out in my dream above everything else. Something I knew I *had* to do to really make this whole shebang work. I need her fear and confusion. I need her begging and pleading. The thoughts already have my heart thudding as I reach my hand out toward the length of her braid. She doesn't stop me, because she has no reason to, letting my hand wrap up it.

"Is that a yes?"

I shake my head at her, watching her lips part when I tug at the braid harder than she anticipated. Her mouth opens in a surprised "O", a hand instinctively slapping onto my wrist to stop my pulling.

"Ow! What... What are you doing?"

I walk with her, forcing her to come with me by my hand in her hair. She turns awkwardly, stumbling along behind me as she tries to push my arms away. She hits me a few times in the back, but I ignore the short ache, shaking her head a bit to disorient her.

"Stop! What're you doing? Stop!"

I tug her along with me to her living room, ignoring her bellows as we go, knowing my silence does nothing but amp up her fear. I throw her into the gray loveseat there, shoving her chest and forcing her back down when she tries to stand. She looks like she might try to stand again, but I shake my head at her. Her confusion and growing fear make her obedient.

"What is happening? Tell me something!"

I bend, eyes on her as I open the drawer of her side table. I pull out a bundle of nylon rope as she frowns, obviously unaware that I had put it there for this moment.

"What is that?"

She tries to bolt, but I stop her, sticking my leg out to trip her. Her hands hit the floor and she cries out, scrambling to get up and away from me. I quickly grab her hair again, yanking her backward. Letting go, I grab her by the waist and turn sideways to try and throw her back into the chair. Her elbow catches my jaw and I grit my teeth, getting angrier with every second this drags on because of her disobedience. Normally I love a good fight, but tonight, I just want shit to go according to plan. She's stopped trying to speak to me, her words replaced with terror-filled yells and bellows.

She grabs onto my arm once I get her back in the chair, her feet coming up to kick me in the gut. They miss only because I move off to the side, gripping one of her wrists to twist it back in an odd angle as I circle the back of the couch. Her screams ring in my ears, nearly blowing my eardrum as I wrench her head back into the loveseat with my other hand. I had dropped the rope in our scuffle, but I'm able to slide it along the floor with my foot, dragging it to me. Releasing her arm but keeping a hold of her hair, I quickly scoop it up. Risking her getting away, I let go of her hair and quickly toss a loop of rope around her middle. She tries to duck under, but I pull it tight, my foot on the back of the loveseat as

I force her to sit. Tying a quick knot, I throw another loop over her, this one squeezing her elbow to her chest so that her hand rests by her face when she tries to wiggle out. The next loop secures her other arm, that one at a more comfortable-looking angle.

Making sure my knots are tight, I walk around the chair, my lungs heaving with the effort that it took. My butterfly is still kicking and yelling, refusing to admit she's stuck. It's admirable really. I hadn't expected her to have so much fight in her. She's still screeching, her screams only stopping long enough for her to draw air into her lungs. I didn't want to have to gag her, but I can't have her waking up the entire neighborhood before I'm finished. Looking around for something to use, I walk back to the foyer and grab her scarf off the hook by the door. I fold it in half as I walk back to my butterfly, quickly wrapping it around her head and tying the ends so that her mouth is covered. You can still hear her, but it's not nearly as loud or ear piercing.

Leaving her alone in the room, I walk through her house to the back, opening the sliding doors onto the patio. Uncovering the barbeque, I grab the bottle of lighter fluid I'd seen here previously, bringing it back into the living room. My butterfly's eyes widen at the bottle in my hand, her legs kicking furiously. She's a smart girl. I'm sure she can see where this is going. Bringing the bottle over her head, I squeeze, the fluid dripping down her hair and shoulders, running over her face so she is forced to squeeze her eyes shut. Her head is shaking back and forth, her body jerking uselessly within her bindings to get free, but I just keep squirting. I spray the fabric of her chair, the floor around her, her side table, the couch, and with the little that's left, her curtains. Tossing the empty bottle onto the floor, I walk over to the coffee table in front of the couch, picking up the candle I'd bought for her last week.

Reaching into my pocket, I pull out my lighter and light it, tucking it back away as I watch the candle flicker in my palm. Watching my butterfly squirm in her seat, listening to her muffled screams, I take out the gold paper butterfly from my pocket and bring it to the flame. This one they won't find. They won't know she's mine, but for some reason that feels okay. Like I don't want them to know about this one. The gold paper starts to smoke, black stink rising before the little paper wing engulfs in flames. I toss it onto the carpet at my *Vanessa carduii*'s feet, watching the carpet quickly light with fire as she raises her legs in an attempt to escape it.

Her efforts are futile, the flames quickly traveling up the sides of her chair and then her legs, the smell of burning flesh and fabric stinking up the room in dark plumes of smoke. I watch the red and orange swarm her body as she shakes her head and listen to the screams leaking through the fabric bound around her head while I stand there holding the candle in my palm. The flames quickly move on to the other objects, wicking like wildfire across the room. It's getting hard to breathe, but I can't get my feet to move, my eyes stuck on my butterfly as she burns in her chair.

I can't feel the heat of the candle in my palm, but I know the glass is warm. The room is also getting unbearably hot. My butterfly stops moving from what I can see through the smoke and flames, so I turn, holding my candle up to the curtain at the edge of the room that has yet to catch on fire. Watching it light up, I drop the candle to the floor and move from the room. Opening the front door, I simply step out, my face immediately burning from the cold sting. I shut the door behind me, my eyes scanning the sleeping street before I start to walk back toward the park.

I know it won't be too long before the fire starts to consume the house and the neighbors wake up. I'm banking on someone to notice and call the fire department. This won't feel complete until I've laid eyes on them. I wander in the shadows of the trees, ears listening for those sirens as I wait. I don't know how long it takes, but they do eventually go rushing by, their sirens blaring, lights almost blinding in the dark. Unable to stop myself, my feet follow them, needing to see things unfold now that they're here.

It hurts to breathe, and my heart is pounding so hard, the anxiousness makes my hands shake. I feel angry despite doing exactly what I wanted. Livid even. It does nothing but confuse me and I find my hands clenching in my pockets as I stomp toward my burning butterfly. I stop when the fire trucks come into view and shift my face off to the side when two police cars go rushing past where I'm standing on the sidewalk. Part of me wants them to see me, wants them to ask if I saw anything, if I know what happened. I almost want to go tell them, a strange nagging in my chest urging to do just that even while my feet stay rooted to the spot by an unseen force telling me they can't know. That they can never know. My mind is warring itself in a way I can't understand.

I did exactly what I wanted. Everything is exactly how it should be, but instead of feeling satisfied, I'm denied once again. But this time it's worse. I can't seem to catch my breath. My fisted hands are shaking so hard inside my pockets that my jacket zipper is jingling under my chin. Shuffling out of view the best I can on the sidewalk, I double over, grabbing my waist as I try to suck in a decent breath. My chest feels like it's caving in, a weight sitting right on my collarbone while my head spins. I don't know what's happening and I don't know how to fix it as my lungs wheeze. A gloved hand slaps onto the fence I'm leaning against, my hunched body shuffling toward the park, my back to the now-raging fire. I almost think I'm having a heart attack with the way my chest is squeezing beneath my palm as I try to jog, back bent so I'm curled in on myself.

Finally making it to the park, I beeline for my car, my lungs slowly starting to gain their ability to suck in air. By the time I get there, I'm standing straight, my heart beating a tiny bit slower than before. I jerk my car door open and fall into the driver's seat, resting my forehead on the steering wheel while I try to keep my breaths steady. My hands are still shaking, trembling in my lap while I squeeze my eyes shut. When I can finally sit up without my vision going blurry, I start my car and pull from the parking spot. I want nothing more than to go home right now. I don't know what this was supposed to prove, why I've reacted this way, but I'm scared to find out.

SIXTEEN

hadley

I don't have to work. When Nana passed, she left me a very large amount of money in her life insurance policy that ensured that I'd be set for a very long time. But sometimes it's boring doing nothing all the time and after meeting Larry, I knew this was the perfect job for me. Twice a month, I go to the Rivercrest retirement home and help with an arts-and-crafts class that they have. I'm sure I stick out like a sore thumb there, but I like it. It reminds me of the many times I spent with my nana, painting stained glass. Dropping my armful of supplies on the front table, I start spreading out different colored watercolor trays and thick paper. Today, we're painting.

Trisha, a CNA who often helps with the crafts, comes through the door, wheeling one of my favorite residents into the room with her. She smiles at me, pushing him to another table. He scowls at me, and I smile in return. "How are you doing today, Larry?"

"I'd be better if they'd let me have another fruit cup with lunch." His shaky wrinkled hands cross over his chest.

"You know we need to watch your blood sugar, Larry." Trisha gives me a side-eye, smirking at me as she comes to stand by the table. "Now what colors do you want? We're going to be painting today."

"I don't want to paint." He huffs at the look she gives him, shaking his head. "Just give me blue."

She chuckles, putting a square of paper, a small plastic cup of water, and a tray of various shades of blue watercolors in front of him. The other residents are starting to file into the room, a few others being wheeled by CNAs like Larry was. It doesn't take long for everyone to settle, and Trisha takes over since she knows I don't like to.

"We're painting today! Hadley brought a bunch of different colors of paint for us to use and you guys can come pick what you'd like."

After everyone has picked their paints and I've done a demonstration on how to paint a silly little rainbow, I walk around the room, making sure no one needs help. Most of the ladies here are crafty themselves and already know how to do most of what we do in these classes, but others, like Larry, struggle a bit. I move to stand near his table, watching as he stares at the giant wet blob he's made.

"That looks interesting, Larry."

He frowns at me, gesturing at his paper. "No. It looks like shit."

I laugh, picking up his discarded paint brush. Dipping it into a lighter shade of blue than he already has, I make a ring around his blob. I walk around the table, reaching for a yellow color palette from the front to make star-like shapes around it. When it resembles an abstract version of the moon and stars, I set his brush down. "There."

His fingers brush along the edge of the paper as he looks down at it. "My granddaughter used to paint." He shifts in his wheelchair, and I wait for him to continue. "She did watercolor."

"I bet it was really pretty."

"It was shit." I laugh again and he smiles, picking up the paint brush to rinse off in the water cup absentmindedly before placing it back down. "But she loved doing it and that's all that mattered."

"You said she used to. Does she not paint anymore?" He shakes his head, the look on his face stopping my heart in my chest immediately, making me wish I could take the words back and pretend I never asked.

"No. We lost Tracy this summer."

I swallow hard. "Tracy? Tracy Mucket?"

"Yes. She took her stepfather's name. Did you know her?"

I suddenly feel sick to my stomach, vomit burning up my esophagus that I have to fight down. "I'm so sorry, Larry. Excuse me, I have to use the restroom." Spinning from the table, I walk as fast as I can from the room without drawing attention to myself. My lungs are on fire as I try to keep my breathing under control. My palm on the doorframe to steady myself, I push into the bathroom and close the door behind me.

I don't understand what's happening. I don't know why the mention of Tracy, someone I don't think I've ever even met, is triggering such a response. Falling forward, I grip onto the sides of the sink, my head bowed as I try and get my breathing under control. My chest is tight, making each breath hard to pull in, my heart beating so hard I can feel it vibrating my ribs.

"... ing News. Tracy Mucket, a senior at Rivercrest University, was found murdered in her own home. Detectives say she appears to be another victim of the Butterfly serial killer. RLQ News anchor, Robert Yunder is currently on the scene..."

Turning the cold water on, I splash my face. It doesn't help. I feel like I'm on fire, my skin burning in hot flashes. My vision is blurring out of focus, black dots dancing when I blink.

Focus!

Focus, Hadley!

Hadley!

"Am I weird, Nana?"

Nana frowns at me over her magazine, curling the edge down with her hand so she can see me properly. "What are you talking about?"

"Am I weird? Brandon Morre said he wouldn't go to the dance with me because I'm weird."

"Yes." She lifts her magazine back up, ignoring my gasp. "What? You asked and I answered."

"That's rude, Nana. You were supposed to make me feel better, not rub it in."

She drops her magazine in her lap and purses her lips. "Honey, you should know by now that you're weird. It's okay to be weird. If anything, it makes you unique. Can you imagine how boring the world would be if everyone living in it was normal?" She lifts her magazine back up, ending our conversation. "Now leave me alone, weirdo. I'm trying to read."

Trisha grabs my arm, lightly shaking me so I look at her. "Didn't you hear the siren? Someone pulled the fire alarm. We have to evacuate."

Now that she's said it, I notice the white-and-red lights blinking on the ceiling and hear the loud wailing. "Yea, sorry, I was just in the bathroom."

"Well, you're out now, so let's go."

SEVENTEEN

hadley

There's knocking on my door, and I look over my shoulder with a frown as I wash the dishes. When they don't just come in, I shake off my hands, grabbing a rag off the counter to dry them. There's another knock before I get there. "Hang on."

Swinging the door open, I blink at Kyler. "What are you doing here? How did you even know my address?"

He shifts in front of the door, looking over my shoulder into the house. "Can I just come in? I just

"Why, is Vickie out of town?" I step to the side, opening the door further for him. "If you came here to fuck, I'm not interested." He shakes his head, walking past me and I shut the door behind us. He stops in the living room, awkwardly looking around. "Well? You wanted to talk, so talk."

His hand raises to his hair, shaking the dark brown strands anxiously through his fingers. "I just... I'm just worried about you, Hadley."

I huff, crossing my arms over my chest, watching his fingers nervously fidget. "Over what? We aren't even friends, Kyler."

"Don't act like that. I've known you since my freshman year at University, Hadley. We might not hang out all the time or talk as often as we used to, but I obviously care about you."

"Yea, whatever. Get to the point, Kyler."

He looks away from me again, his eyes falling on my nana's wind chime. "Were you at the nursing home when the fire alarm went off?"

I run my hand down my arm, frowning at his question. "Yes? Why?"

"Did you do it?" He turns to face me after he asks, his face blank of any emotion that I can read.

I scoff, shaking my head at his ridiculous question. "What? No! Why would I do that?"

His tongue comes out to swipe over his lips, his hand brushing down his face again. "Are you taking your meds?" My lips pinch at his question, the words sinking in my gut. "Don't look at me like that, Hadley. Just answer the question."

"It's none of your business. It wasn't your business when you filled in for one of your dad's pharmacists and it's not now. But yes, I am."

He laughs, like he doesn't believe me. "I don't know that I believe you. Dad said you haven't been by the pharmacy in a while."

I shake my head, my heart thumping beneath my ribs as I walk back into the kitchenette. Dunking my hands in the soapy dishes, I start washing again. "It doesn't matter what you believe. And it's gross and creepy of your dad to be keeping such tabs on me. If all you did was come here to yell at me about something I'm already doing, then you can leave."

"Who's Rhys, Hadley?"

My hand slips on a plate and I almost drop it. "We already had this conversation, remember?"

"I remember. I want you to remind me though. Where is he now?"

I shrug, dropping some silverware into the clean side of the sink. "How would I know? I don't have a tracker on him."

He walks past me, grabbing a black hoodie Rhys left last time he was here that's on the hook, holding it up. "Is this his?" I don't answer and he grabs a pair of sneakers. "Are these?"

Setting more dishes into the sink to rinse, I shrug again. "Yea, they look like his."

He blinks at me, carrying them over to me in the kitchenette. "This is an extra small hoodie and size seven shoe. You think these belong to Rhys?"

I stare at them, my eyes shifting from the things hanging from his fingers to his face. "Guess not. We wear similar things."

He tosses them on the couch, shaking his head like he doesn't understand how I'm not getting what he's trying to say. "Remember when you started running? And I made fun of you for it, saying only losers ran? Why'd you stop running, Hadley? Weren't you driving all the way on the other side of town to see some girl? Why'd you stop seeing her?"

He grabs my arms across the counter, and I freeze, my heart pounding harder with each question. He looks worried as his dark brown eyes search my face. "Did you kill them, Hadley?" I jerk back from him, water splashing onto the floor. He walks around the counter, moving to stand in front of me. "Who's Rhys, Hadley?"

Just as her eyes flutter open under my gaze, I slam her face back into the ground, watching her nose crunch and lips split even more.

I step back from him, but he follows, matching my step. "Who is Rhys, Hadley?"

Her movements are slowing, her limbs looking heavy and weak, but her eyes never close. Those beautiful minty greens stay locked on mine as her arms drop into the water and the last air bubble leaves her parted lips.

My back bumps up against the counter, my lungs burning, my anger making my hands shake. I know who the Butterfly Killer is. "Who is h—"

He looks down at the kitchen knife lodged into his gut, his hands shaking as he steps backward from me. "You're just like everyone else. Pathetic." Gripping the handle, I yank it out, watching Kyler fall back onto his ass. My ears are ringing as I bend down to look into his face. "I didn't kill those girls." He looks like he doesn't believe me, his body shifting backward in a weird crab walk as he tries to get away from me. "I didn't kill those girls!" I kick his legs, dropping down to stab my knife into his thigh. "You know what? You're just like them. All of them. You think I need those pills to be normal, that I can't function like a regular person without them. Well, you're wrong." Ripping my knife out, I slam my knife back into his stomach. I do it again, and again, and again, using his body like the therapy I never had, until his torso is nothing but torn, bloody flesh and my arms are shaking with exhaustion.

Drip. Drip. Drip.

"Put that down and come here, Hadley." My mother's voice calls from the doorway, the silver butterfly clips holding back the hair at her temples, glinting in the light of a candle on the shelf. I ignore her, shaking my head in silent defiance. "Be a good girl and come here."

Drip. Drip. Drip.

A good girl. I snort, lips twisting at my mother. That's not possible. Nothing I ever do is good enough for my parents. I am never good enough for them. My eyes land on my father's unblinking gaze from where I stand near his chair. It's a nice change to not hear him slinging around his insults and disappointment at my behavior. That's all he ever fucking does; all he ever has to say to me. I hear the floorboards creak as my mother takes a step into the room and my attention turns back to her. Her hands are shaking despite the confident bite of her tone just moments ago. Is she scared? What the fuck could she possibly be scared for? I'm the one going to be punished, not her. "Why are you trembling?"

Drip. Drip. Drip.

She ignores my question, her eyes flickering between my hand and my face. "Knock this off right now, young lady!" One of her hands is clutching a pleat in her long skirt, the other gripping the doorframe like she needs the support to keep from toppling over.

Drip. Drip. Drip.

The crease in her brow lightens just a bit when I step forward in her direction, then quickly deepens when she realizes I'm not coming to her. My foot steps into something warm and wet when I pass my father's chair, my toes sticking to the floor as I walk to the candle on the shelf. Letting the hammer I was holding slip through my fingers to my feet, I reach for the candle. The hot glass burns against my palms as I cradle it to my chest, but I don't mind, taking a deep breath to inhale its scent. It smells like sugared donuts, far too pleasant to be in a hellhole like this. I look back at my father, his silent face staring back at me. "No."

I look at my mother. "Do you think I'm crazy?" She stutters, a drop of sweat dripping down her brow. "Do you think I'm crazy?" I scream it at her, making her jump.

"N-n-n… No. You're not crazy, Hadley."

My eyes narrow on her, the tremble in her hands growing. "Then why do you make me take pills? If you don't think I'm crazy, then why did you have Doctor Steven remove my uterus?"

"You had a medical condition. We didn't have a choice." Her eyes keep going to my father, and I scoff.

"I heard you, Mother. I heard you both. You couldn't bear the thought of me, your broken daughter, having children." I'm still holding the candle in my hands, my skin burning the longer it sits. But I don't care, it grounds me.

"You are a vile, evil child, Hadley. You are sick. Your father and I knew you could never be allowed to reproduce. You are not normal. Something is wrong with you!" She screams it at me, getting brave enough to step farther into the room toward my father.

Her outburst almost stuns me silent, my hands trembling so hard the candle almost falls to the ground. I pinch it harder to keep from losing it. "You created me, Mother. What does that make you?"

Eyeing me a moment, she bolts for my father, and I let her, moving to take her place at the door. She trips on the hammer I dropped — the one I used to bust my way into his study — almost falling before she catches on to the arm of his chair. She frantically starts trying to untie him, her feet splashing in the gas that's dripping down from his body and the chair. She rips the binding from his mouth, and I meet my father's gaze over her shoulder. "No!"

I let the candle drop from my hands, the glass bouncing and rolling in the gasoline. It sparks up, a hot rapid path that zips straight to my parents. My mother screams, falling back on her ass as the flames eat her up, my father trying to break from his binds as he wails in agony. I reach into the room, grabbing onto the handle to shut the door. "I am normal."

"I *am* normal!" I scream at his lifeless body, my chest heaving as I stare down at him.

"Hadley."

I startle at the voice, eyes wide as they jump to Rhys standing before me. "It's not what it looks like, butterfly."

My fingers tremble against the knife, blood pooling around my knees as his cornflower eyes sear through my flesh with his anger. "I think we know who the real butterfly is, don't we?"

I shake my head, dropping the knife as I stand in the pool of blood slowly eating up my kitchen floor. "It's not like that. This was an accident."

He laughs, a cruel loud sound that vibrates in my ears. "An accident? How the fuck do you stab someone that many fucking times and call it an accident? Fucking damn it, Hadley!" He steps into the blood, one of his sneakers kicking Kyler's body between us. His hand snaps out, grabbing my cheeks painfully in his palm. "What did I fucking tell you? Huh?" He throws my face away and I stumble backward, catching myself on the edge of the counter. "What did I tell you at the diner?"

He pulls out his phone, angrily dialing while I watch. "If you lose it, we both do." He brings the phone to his ear. "77843 E Redburrow St. You'll find the Butterfly Killer and the newest victim." He ends the call, tossing the phone onto the floor. Any minute now, my house will be swamped with every police officer in Rivercrest Landing. Part of me feels oddly relieved, while the other is screaming. Rhys's hands grab at his hair, his eyes landing on me.

His disappointment burns over my skin like acid, bile rising in my throat. "I didn't kill those women."

His hands drop from his head, eyes narrowing on my face with my admission. "Then who did?"

I swallow, my eyes falling to Kyler's body. "You."

He laughs again, and the sound bounces off the walls. "Bold, coming from the woman who just stabbed her casual fuck to death in her kitchen."

I wait until his eyes find mine, wordlessly begging him to believe me. "Now what?"

He doesn't answer me, red-and-blue lights reflecting in the bright blue of his eyes as he looks over my head and out the bay window.

Looks like I've run out of time.

I watch Rhys as he shakes his head, scrubbing his hands along his face. For a moment, we stand there in the chaos, the indecision thrumming between us like a spider's web. I don't watch as he turns away from me, jogging down the hallway, intent on finding a way out. Instead of following him, I swallow past the nails in my windpipe.

I put myself in this mess and I'll get myself out of it.

I blink with each bang that shakes my door, officers pounding on it while yelling for anyone inside. When I don't answer, it's kicked in, busted at the doorknob. I jump at the loud smack of it hitting the wall, swallowing through a tight throat as I'm met face-to-face with several men as they rush into my house. Sweat drips down my spine as they stare at me, their faces barely hiding their confusion as they take in the scene before them.

Rhys said the Butterfly Killer was here — they're expecting a male, probably him.

The ringing in my ears is clouding their words, making me frown as I attempt to read their lips. "Help me." The words are loud in my head, whispered past my constricted throat as they continue to stare and shout. "Help me." It's even louder, banging around in my brain as I grasp at my only hope for salvation. "Help me!" It's desperate this time, wailing past my lips.

An officer creeps forward and my eyes drop to his booted foot, watching it slap into the blood pooled on the tile. Blurred from the fat teardrops that drip from my chin, one of the officer's hands comes into view, reaching for my wrist as he speaks in a tight voice. "Ma'am what's your name?" I continue to cry, huffing and puffing long enough, he moves to grab me. "I'm going to need you to come with me. Are you hurt? Is this your blood?"

Belatedly, I remember that I'm covered in blood. I can feel it drying along my hands and feel my clothing sticking to my skin where it seeped through. I shake my head and sniffle as I raise my gaze to his, allowing him to walk me toward the door. "No, it's... it's not mine. It's—oh my God, I can't even say it! I can't believe this is real!"

My eyes squint once we step outside, police cars filling my driveway, lights flashing. An EMT runs toward me and the officer gripping my elbow, but I raise my hand, stopping him before he asks any questions.

My voice shakes. "It's not mine, it's my friends. H-he..." I wail into my forearm, my bloody palm on full display as the officer speaks over me to the EMT. After a moment, I'm led to a patrol car where a detective is waiting.

Her hands are tucked into the pockets of her jacket as she observes me, her face hard as she questions the officer now at my back. "Is he in there?" At the shake of his head, she turns her attention on me. "What's your name, ma'am? How'd you end up with all this blood on you?"

Her voice is too sweet for this job. Each syllable that leaves her mouth is as smooth as melted butter. She's pretty too. The lights are bright enough that I can see my own reflection in the brilliant green of her eyes. I almost forget my tears for a moment, looking at her, but then I pull myself together and let my lip quiver once more. "My friend in there, he's… he died." I hiccup back another sob, eyeing her through my tear-stained lashes.

"Alright, we're going to bring you to the precinct. You'll be safe there." She reaches out and pats my arm comfortingly, looking past me to the officer at my side. "Get her cleaned up and warm. We're going to do a search here and see if we can find anything on the guy we're looking for."

I'm promptly shuffled into the patrol car, blinking as the door slams shut. Staring straight ahead, I watch some officers walk around the side of my house and my pulse races, wondering if Rhys was able to get away. I'm joined in the car by two officers, and I sit back, wiping my face with the edge of my t-shirt.

My attention is drawn to the officer in the passenger seat as he looks back at me. "What's your name? Do you live here?"

When I don't answer, he shakes his head, turning back around. My eyes stay latched on my house as we back out, my head swiveling to keep it in my site as we drive away. I don't blink until we've left my street.

EIGHTEEN

hadley

I wrap my hands around the cup of coffee that I'm offered, smiling in thanks. It's warm beneath my trembling fingers, the heat a distraction from the cold room I've been sitting in for the last hour. I was allowed to get washed up; a very drab tan uniform given to me to replace my ruined clothing. I haven't been officially questioned yet, haven't done anything but sit and resist the urge to chew my fingernails.

Please let Rhys be okay.

The seconds tick away on the clock to my right, the noise scratching along my eardrums as

I wait for the ball to drop. Wait for everything to come crashing down. It's only a matter of time now.

The same detective from before enters the room, her back stiff as she smiles at me, smoothing out her crisp white button-up. Her kindness feels forced as she sits across from me, her fingers gently setting a manilla folder onto the metal table between us. "I'm Detective Porter. I don't believe I mentioned that before."

Sipping my coffee, I shake my head in agreement with her statement, the bitter aftertaste making my tongue stick to the roof of my mouth.

Detective Porter's nails lightly drum along the folder as she watches me. "Your name is Hadley, isn't it?"

My back stiffens at the mention of my name, knowing I haven't said it once since being brought in, but I nod, my fingers gripping my paper cup tighter.

"Do you know what happened to Kyler? Why was he at your house?" It's asked casually as she leans back in her seat, her eyes flicking to the two-way mirror on the wall to our left.

I shrug and the cup in my hands shifts, a tiny bit of coffee splashing up and over the rim. "He came to visit and then…" I shudder a breath in my chest and cast a long gaze at the mirror. "It all just went black. I don't know." I look back at her face, feeling a tear work its way from my eye. "I don't know what happened."

She watches me for a moment, her emerald eyes glinting in the bright, buzzing overhead lights. After a moment, she opens her file, and my lungs catch on the flattened origami butterfly she pulls out with delicate fingers. It's a dusty pink, the folds of its wings crisp and pointed. My heart thuds as she holds it up, admiring it for a second before placing it on the tabletop between us. My fingertips burn to touch it, to feel the texture of the paper, but I resist, keeping my hands wrapped around my cup.

"Have you heard of the Butterfly Killer?"

I feel her eyes on me as I stare at the little butterfly, but I don't look up. "A little here and there on the news."

"Only heard of him? You haven't seen him?" My eyes flick up to her face at her tone. "Not even tonight?"

I study her a moment, moving my cup to the side so that I can rest my hands in my lap. "No."

My hand is reaching toward the butterfly, my eyes back on the pretty piece of paper when her voice cuts in, pausing my movements. "I don't think you're telling me the truth." My eyes cut to her, my fingers curling into my palm. "We found this butterfly in your house. And we know you had a hand in killing Kyler." My mouth opens in a rebuttal, but she continues, "Now we have no reason to believe that the Butterfly Killer is more than one person, especially since you made the ph—"

"I didn't make the phone call," I interrupt her, watching her head tilt ever so slightly with confusion.

"What do you mean you didn't call in?"

I don't answer her, not right away, making her sit in the silence as I link my fingers over the table. "I didn't call it in." After a pause, I look at the two-way mirror. "You're not going to get the answers you're looking for."

She lets out a loud breath and ducks her head down for just a moment after I look back at her. "We don't have to be enemies here, Hadley. I just want to understand the situation. Why can't you talk to me?"

I turn my face to look at my reflection once more. "Even if I wanted to tell you, Detective Porter, *I can't.*"

"This is a safe space, Hadley. It's just you and me here." She must see the disdain written on my face because she sighs. "Look, I know that you know who the Butterfly Killer is and maybe even where he is right now. Help me and I'll help you."

My eyes leave the two-way mirror, falling over the detective sitting across from me. She's staring at me expectantly, wishing for an answer I'm not going to give her anytime soon. Or ever. Her eyes drift toward the window, slowly coming back to land on me like she's unsure how to proceed.

She wants me to out Rhys, and that's just not something I'm willing to do.

"Do you know anything about rabbits, Detective?" She shakes her head, but I'm already talking before she's finished. "If a mother rabbit is stressed, hungry, bored, scared, or really many other frivolous things..." I pause, swiping my tongue over my bottom lip to relieve some of the dryness. "She'll eat her babies."

"If you're going to continue to waste my time, I don't see a reason for this talk." She starts to scoot her chair back and I lift my hands from the table, pausing her movements by crooking my finger at her in a come-hither motion.

She tilts her brows in confusion and casts a quick glance at the other officers through the paned mirror. She slowly rises from her chair, her palms flat along the steel surface of the table as she leans toward me. I stand and watch the rise and fall of her chest quickening with the action. Her body instinctively knows it should be wary as I lean forward, my cheek just skimming hers as my lips brush along her ear. "Some people are just born unsettled."

"Wha—"

Her voice is cut off as my hand clamps around her throat, my fingers digging into her soft pale flesh with such force my nails draw blood. I feed off her panic, squeezing harder as her hands grab at mine, her fingernails scratching my skin as she yanks on my arms. They always do that. Panic. There's probably a hundred different ways she could get out of my hold, but when that dark inky fear sinks in, they always lose all rational thoughts in their pathetic little heads.

I hear the shoes squeaking outside of the door, the shouts before they come bursting in, and I tighten my grip on the detective's throat, soaking up her terror for just a few seconds longer. The door bangs against the wall and I'm quickly ripped from the table and thrown backward, my head smacking roughly against the brick at my back. But I don't feel it. All my attention is on the detective and the bloom of pretty little bruises marring her creamy skin.

So fucking beautiful it makes me smile.

She would have made such a pretty, pretty butterfly.

The detective's eyes catch mine for just a moment, a brilliant shade of emerald green brimming with tears. She's coughing, her hand clutching her throat as she tries to regain her composure. I told her she wouldn't get the answers she was looking for. She should have listened.

I'm yanked to my feet by an officer, a pair of cuffs slapped onto my wrists. I have to know if they found Rhys or if he got away. "Did you find the man who made the phone call?"

I watch the rough swallow the detective pushes down, as she nods to the officer checking on her. He backs up and I'm shoved into my chair once more, this time, with an officer at my back. "If you mean the victim, Kyler —"

"I'm not talking about fucking Kyler." The metal of my cuffs ting against the tabletop as my hands tremble, growing angry with her answers.

"There wasn't another person there, a woma —"

"A man called you!" I scream, cutting off her sentence as my fists bang against the table. My heart is beating so quickly I'm starting to feel faint.

The detective holds her hands up, while the other officers step forward at my aggression. She slowly grabs the back of her chair, pulling it back to take her seat again. "I can see we're having a misunderstanding here, and I'm just trying to figure out the facts. You say there *was* another man there?" I grit my teeth as she looks at the officer next to me then back.

My eyes flit around the room, my chest rising and falling at a pace that can't be healthy for someone at rest. Realizing I've said too much, I keep my mouth shut, silently berating my stupidity. I blink at her, my fingers squeezing tightly inside of my fists.

The detective gets up and opens the door to speak to someone in the hall. Moments after returning to her seat, there is a knock on the door, and an officer brings in what looks like a tape recorder. He sets it on the table in front of the detective and she nods to him with thanks before turning her attention back on me. "This is the recording of the call we got at the department earlier this evening." She presses play and before I can even think, the recording starts.

"77843 E Redburrow St., the Butter..."

I don't know what makes me do it, but *something* makes me launch forward to knock the recorder off the table, smashing it into the wall so it breaks apart into pieces. I reach out for the detective, screaming a war cry as I'm ripped back by my ankles. I can't hear that recording. I don't want to know who called. I don't need to hear it. I already know it was my Rhys.

It *was* Rhys, no one else.

My arms are pinned to my sides as I continue to scream, kicking the officer at my back in the shins. Jerking about, I break his hold, sprinting forward to grab at the detective once more. I'm knocked to the ground by an officer, my face smashed into the cold tile as I glare up at Detective Porter. Her eyes are wide as she watches me scrambling about and I can't stop the ugly, barking laugh that leaves my chest. This woman wants to stand there and tear apart my reality, pick at the core of my very existence but *she* is scared?

I'm fucking terrified.

I don't know who I am. I don't have certainty in my future. I am a broken, sad girl whose puppet strings have finally become so tangled, the only choice I have at untangling them is hacking at the frail strings with a cleaver. The one constant I have, the only person I have is on the brink of being ripped from me and I refuse to let it happen.

I *refuse* to let it happen.

"Do you know what it's like, Detective Porter?" I yell it from the floor, my words slightly muffled from the pressure the officer's forearm on my head is applying. "Do you know what it's like to be alone? To exist on this fucking floating rock and not have a single soul that gives a shit whether you live or die? From the moment I was conceived, I was branded insufficient. My oldest childhood memory is of my parents crying. Crying because they didn't know where they went wrong to get me for a child. I've had pills and antidepressants shoved down my throat ever since I could swallow a fucking pill because I was born broken. I needed to be fixed." The officer's forearm leaves my head and I'm yanked up to my knees. "And do you know what, Detective Porter?"

I'm allowed to stand, and she wipes a tear from her cheek, staring at me as I'm shuffled toward the doorway. "What?"

"They were right, Detective. I am broken. I do need to be fixed. I am unsettled." Spinning, I catch the officer at my back off guard, slamming the shard of metal that I'd picked up from the broken voice recorder into the side of the officer's neck. Blood sprays along the mint green of the wall as he scrambles to dislodge it, his mouth gurgling.

I vaguely hear the detective screaming in the background as a gunshot rings out, my shoulder searing with agony. "Don't kill her! Don't shoot! We need her!"

My face is slammed against the wall as I'm grabbed once more, my shoulder screaming in pain as they press their weight into me. I'm slapped with another set of cuffs on my legs as medics scramble toward the bleeding officer in the room. Being pulled up from the wall, I grimace, my eyes latching on to the detective as I'm pushed past her. I'm stomped through the hall in a blur of ugly mint green walls and metal gates, my arm and chest starting to go numb with white hot pain. I barely manage to read the label on the last entrance, *Psychiatric Unit.* People are howling through their doors as we pass, banging and bashing against the walls in a ravenous roar that makes my head pound.

I'm unceremoniously shoved into a room near the end of one of the hallways, my cuffed feet stumbling over themselves as I turn around to watch the officers at my back. One of them grabs my shoulder, digging the cuffs into the skin on my wrists, as I look down at the blood smeared across my hand.

"The staff doctor will come look at your gunshot wound in a bit. Try not to die before then," an officer says at the door, drawing my attention up as he slams it shut and glares at me through the small metal-lined screening window.

In answer, I spit at his face and raise my bloody hand to flip him off.

NINETEEN

hadley

Looking around the small cell, I move to sit on the bed, a hiss leaving my lips when I do. Slowly lying on my uninjured side, I cradle my arm and curl my knees up. I'm exhausted, both mentally and physically, although, it could be the blood loss. I pull my hand away, seeing only a little bit of fresh blood on my hand this time. It seems to be stopping at least. My eyes lift to the overhead lights. I just want to sleep.

"Breakfast is done!" I skip down the stairs, my hand on the banister as I use it to swing around the

corner. Nana is dishing my plate like always and I watch her drop something into my orange juice, stirring it quickly.

"What is that?"

She jumps at my voice, her hand clutching her chest. "You scared me, Hadley!" She waves toward the table, dropping her spoon into the sink.

"What did you put in my drink, Nana?"

She doesn't immediately turn around to look at me, giving me her back as she grabs my cup and plate before walking over to set them on the table. "It was just a vitamin. Stop being so suspicious." She props her hands on her hips and motions her head for me to sit.

"Show me the bottle."

"Oh, will you sto —"

"Now!" Her face pales at my tone, her eyes widening. "Show me the bottle, Nana."

She stares at me a moment, like she's not sure if she wants to keep fighting me on this or not. Eventually, she moves, opening the cabinet with the canned goods. She pulls out a can of carrots, lifting the lid off to pull out an orange pill bottle. She sets it on the counter instead of handing it to me, her eyes staying on the floor as she sets the can on the counter as well.

"You said I didn't need those. You said there was nothing wrong with being different, that it was good to be different."

"It is, honey, but sometimes we need some help and that's okay too."

"You promised!" I step toward her, and she stays put, her eyes finding my face. "You promised you'd never make me take those!"

"Honey."

She grabs onto my arm, and I jerk away, unintentionally throwing her off of me. Her foot slips out from under her, and I see her falling, but don't try to catch her. Her head smacks against the edge of the table with a loud crack, her body slumping to the floor.

"Nana?" I reach out for her, gingerly touching her leg. She barely hit her head. She'll be fine. She has to be fine. "Nana? Please get up." She's all I have.

I wake up to the door being opened and force myself to sit up on shaking limbs. A doctor and three officers come in, the door sliding shut behind them. The doctor speaks first, pushing his glasses up his nose before pulling gloves from his pockets and putting them on. "I'm going to need to cut your shirt to get a better view of your wound, so you're going to need to be restrained."

Running my tongue over my teeth, I nod, slowly shifting back down onto my bed, facing the ceiling. Two officers secure my wrists, hooking my cuffs to the bed with a designated hook. The third secures my feet, the doctor standing back until they're done. They switch places, the doctor moving forward, and I stare at my reflection in his glasses, glaring up at the pale face staring back at me. It feels like an eternity that he pokes and prods at my shoulder, but eventually it's cleaned and sewn shut with a patch taped on top. The doctor leaves the cell first, followed by an officer who comes back with a new uniform that he tosses at my feet while the other unclips me. He eyes me as he removes the cuffs from my feet, indecision painting his features as he reaches for my wrists. I raise them closer to him but give him no comforting gestures that I won't do anything. He pauses only briefly, eyeing the officer that's standing in the doorway staring at me, daring me to make the wrong move. Once my cuffs fall loose, the man in front of me backs away quickly, and I watch all three leave without a single word, locking the cell door behind them.

I hear a shouted, "Lights out," before my cell goes mostly black, a small yellow-hued security light on the wall casting shadows along the floor. Struggling, I pull my ruined shirt the rest of the way off, tossing it onto the floor to replace with my new one. I don't bother with my pants, shifting to move back down on my side. Closing my eyes, I try to banish the thoughts that want to linger about Nana. Of all the things I've done, she's the only one I wish I could take back. She filled a spot in my twisted, tarred heart that could never be replaced. I'm lonely without her. Or at least I was until Rhys. *Now I have neither of them.* I feel a tear leak from the corner of my eye, and I brush it away with my fingers.

"Why are you crying?"

Opening my eyes, I blink to get them adjusted, my heart pounding when they fall on Rhys. I'm confused, my voice a whisper in the dark room. "Because I'm sad." He pushes off the wall and walks over to me, the heels of his sneakers scuffing along the floor as he does. Crouching, he rests his arms on the bed in front of my face and drops his chin to rest on them. "How are you here, butterfly?"

His breath puffs from his lips, licking along the seam of mine as I blink at him. "Don't you get it, weirdo?" He lifts his chin, reaching out to grab the back of my head. He's looking at me like he can see the stars in my dark, like he could this whole time and I was the one who couldn't see his. His lips sink into mine, pressing me into him with reassuring fingertips. Breaking the connection of our lips, he lets me go. "I never left."

COMING SOON
Summer's Camp – A FFM Thriller

BOOKS BY AJ WOLF

<u>Bloody Business Series</u>
Mine
My Heart
My Life
My Girl

<u>Standalones</u>
Wrecked
Chastity (Coming 2021)
Liberated (Coming 2021)
Obsidian Star (Coming Jan 2022)

Halle {also known as AJ Wolf} is a self-proclaimed coffee and wine enthusiast, who loves reverse harem books and is addicted to adopting animals. She digs crows, spooky things, does morning tarot reads and strongly believes in the energies around us. She lives on a small farm with her husband, three children, four dogs, and numerous other critters and livestock.

Follow my socials for the latest updates:

Instagram: @author.halle

Reader Group: Halle's Hellions

www.AJWolfAuthor.com

Printed in Great Britain
by Amazon

71477708R00174